SHERLOCK HOLMES AND THE SHAKESPEARE GLOBE MURDERS

Center Point
Large Print

**This Large Print Book carries the
Seal of Approval of N.A.V.H.**

SHERLOCK HOLMES
AND THE
SHAKESPEARE GLOBE
MURDERS

BARRY DAY

CENTER POINT LARGE PRINT
THORNDIKE, MAINE

This Center Point Large Print edition
is published in the year 2017 by arrangement with
MysteriousPress.com/Open Road Integrated Media.

The text of this Large Print edition is unabridged.
In other aspects, this book may vary
from the original edition.
Printed in the United States of America
on permanent paper.
Set in 16-point Times New Roman type.

ISBN: 978-1-68324-369-4

Library of Congress Cataloging-in-Publication Data
Names: Day, Barry, author.
Title: Sherlock Holmes and the Shakespeare Globe murders / Barry Day.
Description: Center Point Large Print edition. | Thorndike, Maine :
Center Point Large Print, 2017.
Identifiers: LCCN 2017004022 | ISBN 9781683243694
        (hardcover : alk. paper)
Subjects: LCSH: Holmes, Sherlock—Fiction. | Watson, John H.
(Fictitious character)—Fiction. | Private investigators—England—
Fiction. | Murder—Investigation—Fiction. | Large type books. | GSAFD:
Mystery fiction.
Classification: LCC PR6054.A928 S545 2017 | DDC 823/.914—dc23
LC record available at https://lccn.loc.gov/2017004022

For
Basil, Nigel . . . and Charles

CHAPTER ONE

When I entered the sitting room we had shared for so many years, I found Holmes in an attitude I knew well. He was standing impassively by the window, his head wreathed in the smoke from the noxious shag he insisted on stuffing into his old clay pipe. That early morning pipe was invariably made up of the dottle from the previous day, which he carefully kept and dried on the mantlepiece. I have to say it was not one of his more endearing habits and I tried to time my entrance to avoid it. This morning, unfortunately, I was unsuccessful. He made no move to acknowledge my presence but kept his gaze fixed through the parted blinds on the dull grey London street outside.

Knowing that his failure to return my cheerful "Good morning" was due to his absorption rather than any flaunting of the social niceties, I helped myself to the kidneys and bacon Mrs Hudson was in the act of laying on the table and settled down with the morning paper.

"It's good to have you back, Doctor," said that good soul, bustling around to make sure that I had everything I needed. "There are some people who don't notice what you do for them, people who don't let a thing past their lips for days at a time.

Perhaps you can talk some sense into him, for I'm sure I've given up trying."

"Oh, you mustn't worry, Mrs Hudson," I said, "shouldn't be surprised if forgetfulness isn't part of the male condition. My wife says I'm just as bad . . ." I had remarried not too long ago and Mrs Hudson had been prominent among the well wishers.

"And how *is* your good lady?"

"Very well indeed, thank you, Mrs Hudson. Which is more than can be said for her poor old aunt up in Harrogate she's visiting at the moment. I must admit I'd resigned myself to a week or two of boring bachelordom until Holmes's telegram arrived yesterday. The fellow must have second sight. I'd only just waved her off in the cab . . ."

"Had I not had the pleasure of seeing her with my own eyes, I might well have deduced that the present Mrs Watson was a figment of your imagination," said Holmes, turning from the window. "How often has the absence of your better half been the cue for one of our little adventures?"

It was one of my friend's rare attempts at levity and, as such, I welcomed it. It was a pleasing contrast with the Holmes I had encountered on my arrival the previous evening, sitting hunched in his favourite chair by the fire, plucking moodily at his violin.

"Good of you to come, Watson," he said, scarcely

appearing to look up. "I sometimes think you are the one fixed point in a changing universe but I see that even you are not impervious to the stigmata of time and good living."

As we had not seen one another for some months, I determined to indulge him. "Oh, and what tells you that?" I asked.

"Well, you have clearly surrendered some part of your personal toilet to other hands. I suspect to your maid. Your hat was never so well brushed before but the nap is now brushed left to right, whereas you were in the habit of brushing it right to left. In addition, the hat is relatively new and from Messrs Pilditch of the Strand. You, I fancy, never strayed from your old establishment in Jermyn Street since your army days. The nervous tapping of your fingers on your knee tells me that you have recently given up smoking—I assume at your wife's request. And if I'm not mistaken, it's her good plain cooking we have to thank for the extra three—no, two-and-a-half-pounds you have gained since I saw you last.

"Oh, yes, and you have, of course, been much exercised of late about a matter of national importance. You always chew the right hand side of your moustache when you are under stress and the signs are all too recent to be accidental. I toyed with the idea that it might be the latest news from South Africa that was concerning a military man such as yourself, but on the whole I am inclined to put it down to the rather fragile performance of England's middle order batting in the fifth test at the Oval a few weeks ago. And by the way, the thin coating of clay adhering to your left instep is of a type peculiar to the Kennington area—a factor which, I must admit, did tip the balance. I should have a word with your wife's new maid, if I were you."

"Holmes," I said, shaking my head ruefully, having stepped into his snare yet again, "you never cease to amaze me. The way you explain it, a four year old child could work it out."

"In which case, heaven preserve me from four year old children or my simple livelihood will rapidly evaporate." And realising that he had emerged sufficiently from his mood to jest, he threw back his head and laughed in the hearty, noiseless fashion to which I had grown so accustomed.

For the rest of the evening he was his old self, anxious to hear of my recent re-marriage and the ups and downs of my somewhat casual practice. Then, just before we said goodnight, his mood changed again and the brooding look returned. "I owe you an apology, old fellow," he said, "for dragging you here under false pretenses. There is, I regret to say, no bizarre or arcane problem in which I need your valuable assistance. That is the problem in a nutshell.

"Oh, there are cases, to be sure, but none that

keeps boredom at bay for more than a moment or two." He named one or two that I remembered reading about in the papers in recent weeks. "Insults to the intelligence, Watson, insults to the intelligence and do you know something? I may be becoming paranoid but I swear people are beginning to copy our cases for their crimes. You recall the affair of the Blue Carbuncle, where the thief hid the purloined jewel in the crop of a Christmas goose? Well, where do you think the Duchess of Albermarle's pendant came to light? Stuffed, rather inelegantly, into the turkey. The butler did it, of course.

"Life is fast becoming uninterrupted *déjà vu*, Watson. You know my life has been one long battle with boredom, which you have time and again helped me keep at bay. Yet, I can feel *ennui* reaching out its withered fingers to embrace me. I have even been driven to considering the pipe of late . . ."

Seeing my start of surprise, he laughed again briefly. "Oh, don't worry old fellow, I left the seven per cent solution behind me many a year ago. As you yourself pointed out many a time, it *was* no solution. I mention it merely to indicate the depths of my boredom.

"No, I must confess I lured you here entirely for the pleasure of your company, knowing that you were temporarily at liberty. I thought we might do some long-avoided cross-indexing for want of anything more diverting. And, frankly, I had the rather superstitious hope that your presence within the old quarters might re-create the chemistry for crime." And here he gestured at the maze of Bunsen burners and retorts that were his world when all else failed.

Soon after we turned in and this morning I was pleased to see he seemed more like the Holmes I knew. The glint was back in the eye and his movements were energetic rather than restless.

"Well, Watson," he said, spearing the last piece of bacon that I had mentally consigned to my own plate, "if you've quite finished sustaining the inner man, perhaps Mrs Hudson will be good enough to clear away the debris. I never think it gives a client the right impression when they're asked to pour out their problems over congealing crockery."

"What makes you think you'll *have* a client?" I asked, somewhat grumpily. With rare exceptions, Holmes was in the habit of using food as fuel, whereas a well-cooked rasher of bacon never failed to receive due appreciation from me.

"Because I was watching her from the window while you and Mrs Hudson were cataloguing my shortcomings. And if I'm not mistaken, that will be her at the door now." Indeed, as if on a cue in a melodrama, there was a hesitant ring at the front door below. Hastily gathering the breakfast things together, Mrs Hudson hurried off to answer it.

Holmes took up residence in his favourite chair by the fireplace, his fingertips steepled in front of his face and his eyes to the ceiling, his long legs stretched out in front of him.

"An actress without doubt. Not a particularly successful one or else fallen on hard times. American at a guess or, at the very least, she has been out of this country for some time. Oh, and her clothes are not her own. Interesting . . ."

"Come, Holmes," I said impatiently, "you know how your little games upset me until I know the answers. Speak up, man—how can you possibly know that?"

"My dear fellow, it's rather hard to draw any other conclusion when you have watched a woman pace up and down the pavement opposite for fully five minutes, mouthing to herself and gesturing, then doing the same thing with different gestures. That is the behaviour either of a lunatic or of an actress learning her lines. And I have felt that there have been occasions in the theatre lately when there was little to choose between the two! Then, when she did decide she was ready to make her entrance, she looked at the traffic the wrong way—a habit which bespeaks someone who has spent time on the continent of Europe or, more probably, in the land of our lost colonies . . ."

"And the clothes?"

"It has been my observation over the years that ladies who wish to consult me invariably take great pains with what they wear. They appear to be under the illusion that fine clothes will compensate for what is all too often a thin story. They feel more confident when they know they look their best, yet this lady kept tugging at her clothes, from which I deduce that, either she is not used to wearing finery or that they are not her own. Ah, here she is now . . ."

"Miss Adler to see you, Mr Holmes." Mrs Hudson had been about to say more but was clearly taken aback—as I was—by Holmes's reaction. Our visitor's arrival had found him rising to his feet but the announcement of her name froze him into position for a moment, like a large bird poised for flight. I knew immediately what was going though his mind.

Could this tall woman standing in our doorway, dressed from head to foot in black, her face covered with a thick veil, possibly be *Irene* Adler—the woman, the only woman ever to defeat Sherlock Holmes, as she had in the affair of a Scandal in Bohemia some years earlier?

Seconds later the question was resolved. Moving across the room towards him, precisely like an actress making her stage entrance, the lady offered Holmes the fingertips of her gloved hand.

"Mr Holmes, I presume? My name is Flora Adler, daughter of Florenz Adler, the theatrical impresario. You may know of him?"

Holmes bowed and nodded, his composure

completely regained. Never having met him before, it was quite probable that Miss Adler had not detected the signs that were obvious to Mrs Hudson and myself. Holmes himself was no mean actor. In fact, I have often reflected on what the stage lost when he devoted himself to the theatre of crime. As he showed her to the visitor's chair, I consigned the coincidence to the back of my mind but, as I reflect on it now, I wonder whether that momentary shock did not somewhat dull my friend's razor sharp senses at the outset of what turned out to be one of the more complex cases he was ever to engage in?

"Indeed, Miss Adler, who has not heard of the great showman who staged Wagner's *Ring* in the Grand Canyon, transformed Times Square into a temporary circus—though I'm told many people found your father's animals infinitely preferable to its normal denizens—and organised a chariot race around Central Park? Not to mention introducing America to European opera and ballet almost single-handed. And now I hear he has crossed the Atlantic to colonise us?"

At that moment some pieces fell into place for me, too. I snatched up the morning paper and riffled through it until I found the story I'd been reading when Holmes interrupted my morning ritual. "Ah, here it is," I interrupted. "Adler. Isn't he the fellow who's rebuilding some Elizabethan theatre down on the river?"

"Not *some* Elizabethan theatre, Watson—*the* Elizabethan theatre. Shakespeare's own playhouse—the Globe—and within a few yards of where the scholars seem for once to agree the original must have stood. If I'm not mistaken, Miss Adler, your father proposes to open it very shortly and in the presence of Her Majesty the Queen?"

"That's right, Mr Holmes," she replied and then to our considerable surprise from behind her impenetrable veil came the sound of loud sobbing. I immediately leaned forward to offer her my bandana but she held up her hand in a gesture of refusal and rummaged in her purse until she found a delicate cambric handkerchief, which she raised to her eyes, still without lifting her veil.

Holmes, always adept at allowing his lady clients to regain their composure, continued. "But surely, Miss Adler, this should be an occasion for rejoicing not tears? That your father should be so close to achieving something which many men have dreamed of for the past three hundred years must be the crowning success of even his—shall I say exceedingly 'dramatic' career. That it took an American to restore to the world the platform its greatest writer peopled with *Hamlet*, *Othello*, *King Lear*, *Julius Caesar* and so many others is, I freely confess, something which should make an Englishman feel somewhat inadequate. But that temporary embarrassment should take nothing away from what your father is on the brink of giving to us all."

I turned again to the paper. "And it says the opening performance is only a few days away." Here I read aloud from the report:

"The theatre is already fully booked for the gala occasion. Some one thousand, five hundred people will pack themselves into the three covered galleries or stand around the stage as 'groundlings', just as their Elizabethan forebears used to do.

American impresario, Florenz Adler, however, has managed to achieve something the original Globe could not boast. At the opening, September 21st, 1899 the performance will be graced by the presence of HM Queen Victoria, whereas Queen Elizabeth—keen supporter of the players though she was—is thought never to have visited the playhouse, preferring to summon them to perform at Court."

"Quite an honour, eh, Holmes?"

"Yes, but that's just it," Miss Adler cried, sounding, if anything, even more distressed. Then, with a supreme effort, she managed to calm herself. "I'm sorry, gentlemen. I'm sure I don't seem to be making too much sense. It's just that I'm so worried about my father."

Holmes sat back in his chair, giving off that air of calm I have known to relax the most agitated of visitors. "Miss Adler," he said in a low tone, "Dr Watson and I are at your service. Please proceed with your story. Are you sure you will not remove your veil? As you wish."

"Well, Mr Holmes, I'll try and tell it as simply as I can but I fear there are terrible forces at work. A man like my father, as I'm sure you can imagine, does not rise in his profession without making enemies. Nor is he an easy man by temperament. He does not suffer fools and I'm afraid his definition of 'fool' is a broad one. He has always been fiercely competitive and many of his rivals have been left along the way. Over the years there have been threats, abusive correspondence . . ."

"And what has been your father's reaction?" asked Holmes.

"Oh, he'd just laugh and tear them up and say something like—'People who can't stand the heat should get out of the kitchen!'"

"A curious language," Holmes murmured, almost under his voice. "Pray continue."

"There seems to be something about this project that's bringing things to a head. He knew when he started that a lot of people would be jealous and so it's proved. There have been articles in the newspapers. What right has an American to tamper with our national heritage? That sort of thing. You must have seen them, Mr Holmes?"

My friend inclined his head, unwilling to interrupt her flow.

"But it's the strange *letters* . . ."

"What is so strange about these as opposed to the other letters, Miss Adler? I beg you to think carefully." Holmes was now all attention, leaning forward in his chair, his fingers laced.

"Well, they're not exactly *letters*. Just type-written notes with quotations on them and unsigned. Oh, and they all have a drawing of a rose at the bottom of them."

"Do you have any of these notes?" Holmes asked, stretching out a hand.

"My father threw them away. He said he wasn't going to waste his time dealing with a crackpot But I did manage to retrieve the most recent, which only arrived this morning." At this Miss Adler began to fumble awkwardly with her purse and finally produced a folded scrap of white paper, which she handed to Holmes. He then proceeded with the ritual I had seen a thousand times, holding it up to the light, feeling the texture, even smelling it before he unfolded and read it.

While he did so, the silence in the room was palpable. "What do you make of it, Holmes?" I said finally, more as a means of breaking it than with any real expectation of an explanation.

"I doubt that we are *meant* to make much of it,"

he replied, handing me the document. "Typed on paper that can be bought in any stationer's by someone who is left handed and unaccustomed to using a typewriter. You can see by the way he— or she"—and here he looked at Miss Adler— "puts more pressure on the letters 'e,' 'a,' 'r,' 's,' and 't' which occur on the left hand side of the key board. No, the 'style' is as clear as that of a concert pianist performing a particular piece. I have written a short monograph on 'Crime and the Language of Typewriters' since I saw you last, Watson. There are, in fact, a dozen other aspects to be observed but that will suffice."

I looked at the note properly for the first time and took in its content. There typed in the middle of the page was the quotation Miss Adler had spoken of . . .

FIRST I BEGAN IN PRIVATE WITH YOU, MY LORD OF LINCOLN
Henry VIII

And then, in the bottom right hand corner as a kind of signature, a tiny freehand drawing of a rose.

Holmes was concluding. "And other than the fact that I very much doubt the writer is an amateur horticulturalist, I can deduce nothing else for the moment. And so, Miss Adler, what is it that you wish me to do for you?"

"Talk to my father, Mr Holmes. Beg him for all our sakes to give the project up. If you could have seen the other notes. Although they said nothing specific, they all had this strange threatening tone. I'm convinced we're dealing with someone who means real harm to him and he'll never listen to me. Oh, won't you please help?"

"Well, it does have certain bizarre aspects but then—as Watson will confirm—it has been my experience that the more bizarre a thing appears, the less mysterious it usually proves to be. Perhaps we are looking at an exception here. Miss Adler, I will certainly consider your case. If you will be good enough to leave the note with me and return at the same time tomorrow, I will give you my decision. Good day."

At this he rose and held out his hand, causing her to rise in turn. She, clearly surprised—as was I—to find the interview over so abruptly, barely touched his fingers in farewell and made for the door.

"Oh, and Miss Adler . . ." Holmes quietly addressed her retreating back. She seemed to pause a moment before turning.

"Yes, Mr Holmes?"

"If there should be any more notes, you will be sure to bring them, won't you? And please don't handle them any more than you have to."

She nodded and with that, she was gone.

"I say, Holmes," I couldn't help expostulating,

"weren't you a little abrupt with the young lady? After all, she is understandably anxious about her father's well-being."

"You may be right, old fellow. The ladies have always been your department and there is something about this one . . . She has done her homework on us, now let us do ours on her." By now he was standing once again by the window. "While I watch her make her exit, will you be so good as to look up *Adler, Florenz* in my American index?

"Ah, yes, as I thought—she has played the part she came to play. She is clearly relieved. Strange— her step should be lighter and yet it seems heavier, if anything. Still the veil . . ."

"Probably afraid one of her father's friends will see her visiting Sherlock Holmes," I offered.

"Possibly, Watson, possibly—and yet . . . Ah, you've found the entry. Good man."

He took the bulky volume from me and ran his finger down the entry. "Florenz Adler. Born Chicago, Illinois 1830 . . . hmm, let's see . . . early career as an actor . . . appearances include . . . here we are, Watson, one of the pieces of the puzzle in our hands right away . . . our friend Adler had a small part in a play called *Our American Cousin*. Does that ring any bells, Watson?"

"Nor a solitary peal, I'm afraid, old fellow. Should it?"

"I know your usual playgoing is somewhat

limited to the music halls but I thought it might have appealed to your sense of history. *Our American Cousin* was the play being performed at Ford's Theatre, Washington the night President Lincoln was assassinated by a fellow actor, one John Wilkes Booth. April 14th 1865.''

"Good heavens, the quotation—'My Lord of Lincoln'.''

"Precisely, Watson. 'First I began in private with you . . .' Which presumably means that if the private warning doesn't work, something more public will follow.''

"But what about the rose?''

"That, I confess, eludes me for the moment—although I believe we may safely set aside the possibility of a resumption of our own Battle of the Roses. The answer to this may now lie on these shores but I am fairly sure that its origins lie in the so-called United States of America. I fancy the next note will tell us more.''

"The next note?'' I looked at Holmes with surprise. "What makes you think there'll *be* a next note?''

"My dear Watson, I'd be prepared to wager you a pound of your favourite tobacco—since I know you won't touch mine—that the game is just beginning. Miss Flora Adler struck me as someone playing the part of the concerned daughter and we have to ask ourselves why.''

"Why *what,* in heaven's name? The girl's

presumably picked up some theatrical mannerisms. You know what these actors are like. They never know when they're acting or when it's real."

"Dear old Watson," Homes laughed. "My point precisely. So why hide your most dramatic performance behind a veil where no one can see it? And one more thing. As I have pointed out on more than one occasion, the key to observing a man is the trouser knee and with a woman it is invariably the sleeve that gives the important clues. To that I am now inclined to add the gloves . . ."

"The gloves?"

"Yes, the gloves. Have you ever known a woman who did not remove her gloves in company? Even when she was fumbling in her purse to find the paper, Miss Adler steadfastly refused to do so, even though doing so would have simplified her task considerably. And did you notice that, although I made a point of going to shake her hand, she gave me no more than her fingertips and those were shaking as though she had the palsy. And yet, as soon as she was outside in the street, she couldn't wait to tear the gloves off and drop them into a nearby bin.

"My dear Boswell, I do believe it may be time for you to dust off your foolscap and sharpen your quill or whatever you use. I have a distinct feeling that the game may be afoot."

CHAPTER TWO

As he thrust the volume back among piles of apparently scrambled papers, Holmes kept up that tuneless humming that always signified a contented state of mind in him. Once again there was something to keep boredom at bay. For something to say—for I knew there was nothing to be gained by further questioning—I commented on the random nature of his filing system.

"A deliberate attempt to confuse mine enemies, old fellow," he laughed. "Even Moriarty, the Napoleon of Crime, would, I fancy, have confessed himself beaten when faced with it! Pass me that bust, would you, to hold these papers down?" I handed him the small plaster head of Shakespeare he indicated, a souvenir of an earlier case. Holmes weighed it thoughtfully in the palm of his hand. "I begin to wonder whether we might not be dealing here with the *Shakespeare* of Crime, Watson. Yes, Mrs Hudson . . . ?"

"A note for you, Mr Holmes," said that good lady, handing it to him as she entered the room. "And there's a young man downstairs, very well dressed, says he's to wait for your reply."

Tearing open the envelope, Holmes scanned the contents rapidly. "We seem to be in the market for cryptic messages today, Watson. This one is from my brother, Mycroft. He asks me to call upon him as a matter of some urgency. And since Mycroft is parsimonious with his words, we must assume that this use of the word 'urgency' speaks volumes and certainly no less than the end of civilisation as we know it. Come, Watson, you may well be needed. Mrs Hudson, tell the young man we are on our way."

Five minutes later we were bowling along in a hansom towards Pall Mall. I had no need to enquire as to our destination. Mycroft Holmes, my friend's elder brother, seldom stirred far from the confines of the Diogenes Club, an institution he had helped to found and once described to me by Holmes as being for the convenience of the most unsociable and unclubbable men in town. You could pass its portals and be totally unaware of its existence, a fact which pleased its members mightily, insofar as anything was known to please them.

Holmes's prediction appeared to be well founded, since we found Mycroft pacing the lobby of the club's somewhat dingy premises, almost filling it with his bulk.

I had met him occasionally over the years and indeed he had been involved personally in the cases which my readers may remember as The Greek Interpreter and the Bruce Partington Plans. Holmes, I knew was fond of his brother in his own undemonstrative way and I had observed the feeling to be reciprocated. It was Mycroft, for instance, in whom he had confided after the affair at the Reichenbach Falls, when the whole world—myself included—had believed him to be dead, pitched over the falls in a death struggle with Moriarty. At the time I had been greatly disturbed to think that *I* should not have been the recipient of that confidence but, as usual, Holmes's judgement had been the correct one. I am, as he has often told me, given to wearing my emotions on my face and my evident grief was an essential part of his cover.

In the intervening years, I had come to know Mycroft somewhat, though I doubt anyone could claim to know him well. Those few who were familiar with his name were under the impression that he had some minor government position, though Holmes always insisted that his brother was "the most invaluable man in the country." "I promise you, old fellow, that his brain, once motivated, leaves mine far behind. It is as well for the criminal classes that Mycroft is congenitally idle. If crime could be solved from a club armchair, he would be the greatest criminologist who ever lived." This, then, was the caged lion pacing in his lair of the Diogenes Club.

On second thoughts, a caged bear would have been nearer the mark. Massive was the word that came first to mind when describing Mycroft Holmes. Bigger than his brother in every way, he seemed to bear little resemblance until one came to look at the eyes. Both men had that intent, faraway gaze that seemed to take in everything there was to see and then to look beyond.

After that, it was possible to discern a certain similarity in the facial expression, a certain sharp watchfulness, as if they were constantly on their guard. I should not have cared to play any game of chance with either one of them. My army pension suffered enough from the unpredictability of horse races at it was.

No sooner had we crossed the club's threshold than Mycroft had a huge hand around both our shoulders and was steering us out again and across the street towards the set of rooms he maintained just opposite. Had I attempted the feat myself, I should undoubtedly have incurred the wrath of numerous cabbies for crossing their path without looking. Somehow sensing Mycroft's purpose, they gave him a wide berth. "Thank you for being so prompt, Sherlock. Good to see you again, Doctor. Forgive me for not observing the usual courtesies."

"My dear Mycroft, when did you *ever* observe the usual courtesies?" Holmes laughed and received a grunt for the intended pleasantry.

Moments later we were up the short flight of steps and ensconced in the luxuriously shabby comfort that seemed so appropriate to a confirmed bachelor who took in everything except his immediate surroundings. Holmes and I refused his offer of a whisky and soda—it was, after all, barely eleven o'clock—but Mycroft poured himself a substantial brandy before settling himself in his favourite armchair to state his business.

Before he could begin Holmes said, "Perhaps it would save time, Mycroft, if you were to tell us which Shakespearean quotation a certain lady has received?"

I must admit my own jaw dropped but if Mycroft was surprised, the only indication of it was the miniscule raising of one eyebrow and perhaps the slight tightening of a jaw muscle. Then he broke the momentary silence and said, rather coldly I thought: "I am surprised the Prime Minister has been to see you. I thought we had agreed that I should be the one to handle this somewhat delicate matter. I gave him my considered opinion that a visit from the Marquess of Salisbury to Mr Sherlock Holmes would be enough to set the gentlemen of the public press off sniffing and baying."

"Set your mind at rest, Mycroft and forgive me my little subterfuge. You know I can never forebear to disturb the placid surface of your composure in some small way. Poor old Watson is the usual beneficiary of my mischievous turn of mind.

"The reason I assumed the involvement of— you know the lady to whom I refer—is because I am well aware of the role you have long played in her closest council. As to the Bard—if you, who are more likely to pore over *Hansard* or a balance sheet, choose to leave a copy of Mr Bartlett's excellent *Concordance to Shakespeare* lying around, what else am I to deduce but that you are attempting to trace a quotation? And after the experience Watson and I have had earlier this morning, deduction turns into certainty . . ."

With that Holmes related the circumstances of Flora Adler's visit and the implied threat to her father. Mycroft listened to his brother, demonstrating all the emotion of the legendary graven image. His brandy finished, he put his fingers together in front of his face and then one could see the fraternal resemblance. The story over, he nodded once.

"I wish I could say your tale of thespian rivalry put my mind at rest, Sherlock, but I cannot rid myself of the whiff of brimstone. A threat to a controversial competitor has a certain perverted logic to it but this raises more serious questions . . ."

And here he hauled himself from his chair, crossed to the table on which Holmes had observed the book and extracted from its pages a folded piece of paper that looked all too familiar. Silently, he handed it to Holmes, who took it and examined it from every angle before attempting to read its contents.

"Notepaper identical in type, even though the

type is too common to be helpful," he murmured, as if to himself. "The 'accents' in the typing itself, however, once again speak to us louder even than the words. Yes, this is undoubtedly from our floral friend. Now, what does he have to say . . . ? Ah, *Richard II*? Royalty speaks to royalty. What do you make of this, Watson?" And with that he passed the note to me.

There was the drawing of a rose and above it . . .

COME ON, OUR QUEEN; TOMORROW
WE MUST PART. BE MERRY.

Richard II

"Good heavens, Holmes. Does it mean what I think it means? Is this lunatic threatening to kill the Queen?"

"When you have eliminated the impossible, which we have yet to do, what remains—as I have said so often—however improbable, must be the truth. And the truth would seem to be that we are meant to think precisely that," Holmes replied thoughtfully.

"And that, indeed, is a possibility we—that is, the Palace," Mycroft caught himself, "are taking very seriously indeed. There is, as you must know, gentlemen, a certain amount of incipient civil unrest at the moment. Not against Her Majesty personally, but on account of the

31

worsening situation in South Africa. I fear outright hostilities there cannot be long deferred and there are hotheaded elements here at home who might well contemplate a subversive act, particularly of a theatrical nature, to undermine national morale. Her Majesty has been most strongly advised to abstain from public appearances for the next few weeks, until we can take a more considered view . . ."

"And what was the lady's reaction to that suggestion?" Holmes interrupted.

"I'm afraid she was not amused," said Mycroft with what in a lesser man would have passed for a twinkle in his eye, which was gone in even less time than it took me to detect it. "She apparently expressed the further view in private that she had had quite enough of being compared to a certain other female monarch and had every intention of fulfilling the specific duty in which that predecessor had been notably derelict. The subject was then declared firmly closed."

There was a moment's silence while we all digested that information. I was the first to speak. "But the opening of the Globe is only a few days away!"

"Which is why I asked you to come here today." Mycroft replied, turning to Holmes. "We—and I speak here for the Prime Minister and the whole of the Cabinet—would like you to look into these letters and see if there is a real threat to the

Crown or are they just a form of bizarre poison pen activity? Time, I need hardly add, is of the essence."

And then, before Holmes could answer, the gleam returned to Mycroft's eye. "Of course, this is your area of expertise in which I can only consider myself a poor and occasional player but I feel sure it has not escaped your notice, Sherlock, that 'Flora' is the Latin word for flower."

Anxious to make a contribution to the conversation—and just in case my friend had missed the connection—I found myself declaiming:

Full many a flower is born to blush
  unseen,
And waste its sweetness on the desert air.

In the silence that followed I added—"I remember being made to learn that at school."

As we were outside hailing a passing hansom a few minutes later, Holmes murmured: "I think you'll find that's Gray, old fellow, not Shakespeare. Nonetheless, the sentiments remain admirable."

"Where to now, Holmes?" I asked, ready to change the subject. By now a hansom was drawing up beside us.

"Why, to the great Globe itself, where else?" he replied, stepping inside.

Just as I was on the point of following suit,

a paperboy seemed to appear out of nowhere. Before I had a chance to say anything, he had thrust a newspaper into my hand and hurried off. By the time I had settled myself beside Holmes and the cab was under way, I was quite flustered. "Did you see the infernal cheek of the fellow? Practically knocked me over and I didn't even *ask* him for a paper . . ."

"Nor did he ask you for any money," Holmes pointed out. And so saying, he leaned across and practically tore the offending newspaper from my hands!

"I say, Holmes, there's no need for you to copy his behaviour," I protested.

"If you'll look back, Watson, you may be just in time to see our 'paper seller' turning the corner of Stafford Street and the pile of papers lying at the foot of the railing. I'd be prepared to wager that yours was the only paper he 'sold' today—which is why I am curious to see what is so special about this 'special edition'."

"I can't get over his extraordinary behaviour," I went on. "Never known a paperboy like it."

"Had he *been* a paper boy, I should be forced to agree with you, Watson, but he was no more a paperboy than either of us. I'm afraid you saw but you did not observe. You saw a man carrying a bundle of newspapers. Ergo, he was selling papers. And since few people are in the habit of studying paperboys, any more than they are of scrutinizing postmen, that is all you took in.

"Tell me, have you ever seen a paper seller in Pall Mall?" I had to admit that I couldn't recollect doing so. "Precisely, my dear chap. And should any venture in that direction, they would be firmly deterred from plying their trade in such close proximity to the Diogenes Club, which prefers its papers—like everything else—to be delivered discreetly through the back door. And again, when have you ever seen one who wore an ulster, particularly on a warm autumn day like today? That was to conceal his true purpose while he loitered."

"Was there anything else that I missed while the ruffian was molesting me?" I asked somewhat huffily.

"Only what he said." Holmes by now was busy shaking the pages of the paper.

"What he *said?*"

"Yes, to add verisimilitude to his performance he attempted to emulate the cry of the paper seller. If I'm not mistaken, he shouted something like—'British Position in South Africa Worsens. Read All About It!' "

"And that was all?"

"Yes, but more than enough to tell us that the fellow hails from North America—either Canada or, more probably, one of the north-western states. He turned 'British' into something closer to 'Briddish'. It was faint but it was there. And there was no mistaking his pronunciation of 'aboot' for 'about'. Once more, the American Connection. One of these days I must write a short paper on the subject. I may call it 'Convicted from His Own Mouth.' Perhaps you will remind me . . . ah, I thought so . . ."

A small fold of paper had fallen to the floor of the cab. Holmes immediately picked it up and ignoring his usual ritual, began to study its contents. "Let's see what our friend has to say to us . . ."

Looking over his shoulder, I read it with him. In every way it was identical to the other two notes, except that this one had two quotations. The first one on the cover of the fold read:

WE THREE, TO HEAR IT AND END IT BETWEEN THEM
The Merry Wives of Windsor

"We are now, I'm afraid, firmly cast as characters in his plot, Watson, whether we like it or not. I must admit, my regard for him is beginning to increase. He might easily have settled for 'When shall we three meet again . . . ?' but, fortunately, our friend does not appear to lack a sense of humour as well as a textual knowledge. What else does he have to say?"

On the inside of the note was a second message . . .

MORE THAN WORDS CAN WITNESS,
OR YOUR THOUGHTS CAN GUESS.
The Taming of the Shrew

"A challenge, Watson, I do believe—a challenge."

And then that infuriating man tipped his hat over his eyes and proceeded to sleep for the rest of the journey with a smile on his lips.

CHAPTER THREE

I must admit that the report in the morning paper had not prepared me for the sight of the new Globe. Frustrated in his determination to build on the site of the original Globe by the prior claims of a brewery, a terrace of Georgian houses and—most permanently—by the traffic flowing over the major thoroughfare of Southwark Bridge Road, Florenz Adler had once again thought on a large scale. If he couldn't have the original site, he'd have a *better* site. By the simple expedient of buying a row of busy warehouses and tearing them down, Adler's Globe was actually on the river enjoying a nodding acquaintance with St Paul's on the opposite bank.

What he had built was spectacular. Rising three stories high, part timbered and part plastered in gleaming white, it was capped with a roof of thatch, the first permitted in London (the writer informed me) since the Great Fire of 1666.

I became aware of Holmes saying something. "But pardon, gentles all, the flat unraisèd spirit that hath dar'd on this unworthy scaffold to bring forth so great an object."

"Oh, I don't know, Holmes," I said, "I wouldn't call it unworthy at all. Looks absolutely first rate to me."

"Nor would I," Holmes smiled, "It was Will Shakespeare who did and he was, I suspect, being ironic. Can you imagine what it must have been like in his day to be standing outside the Globe, waiting to enter a world of magic? Ladies and gentlemen, scholars and scribes, cutpurses and courtesans, every level of society mingling here 'to hear a play', to feel a part of the performance. Watson, I fear that in our more ordered times we may well have sacrificed something of inestimable value. Let us see what awaits us inside the 'wooden O' . . ."

Picking our way through the builders and the debris that always appears to be infinitely more than the largest structure can possibly generate, we walked through a passage way and suddenly found ourselves once more in the open air with the warm September sun causing us to shield our eyes.

Rising around us were three covered wooden galleries, enclosing us like a hand. Jutting halfway into the unfinished yard was the stage, almost at head height with its brightly painted roof supported by two enormous marble columns, which I later learned were, in fact, painted wood. Despite the noise of sawing and hammering, it took the breath away with its grandeur.

This time it was a woman's voice that brought me back to reality. It was as if she were answering my friend's earlier soliloquy or perhaps continuing it . . .

" 'Piece out our imperfections with your thoughts . . . for 'tis your thoughts that now must deck our kings' . . . I couldn't help overhearing you quoting from *Henry V* as you came into the theatre, sir. It's just about my favourite speech in the whole of Shakespeare. But I'm being very rude. May I introduce myself? My name is Carlotta Adler. My husband, Flo, is responsible for all this, I'm afraid." And here she opened her arms wide in an unashamedly theatrical gesture to take in the whole of the Globe.

It was something in that gesture that triggered a long forgotten memory. Carlotta . . . ? Carlotta . . . ? "Carlotta *Montevecchio!*" I exclaimed for, despite Holmes's teasing, he knew perfectly well that I enjoyed the opera as well as he did. In point of fact, we'd spent many an evening at Covent Garden or the Albert Hall and during those empty years after the Reichenbach episode the image of my friend that recurred most frequently was of his rapt expression as the music enveloped us and of his long, elegant fingers keeping time to it.

"Quite right, Watson," Holmes interrupted my reverie. "Carlotta Montevecchio, known to her considerable public as 'The Neapolitan Nightingale'. If I'm not mistaken, we saw her together on her farewell tour in—1882, was it not—shortly before my enforced absence? After which the world of opera lost a major jewel from its crown." He took her hand and, to my surprise, bent and kissed it. "Now, Miss Montevecchio—I beg your pardon, Mrs *Adler*—permit me to introduce myself. I am Sherlock Holmes and this is my friend and associate, Dr James Watson."

I shook the lady's hand as firmly as a growing shyness would permit. Holmes is fond of deferring to me as a ladies' man and I suppose over the years I have had my moments but here was I face to face with a legend, one of the most glamorous divas of modern times. And although the lady must be well into her fifties, the fineness of her features and the erectness of her carriage were unimpaired. Carlotta Montevecchio in the flesh remained the goddess she had always been on the stage. Then the goddess spoke.

"Mr Holmes," she said, "the honour is all mine. Who does not know of your successes? I had better own up to my guilty secrets before you discover them for yourself." One look at her heightened colour and the sparkle in her eyes (which I now saw to be a bewitching shade of violet) told me that Holmes had awakened a sense of herself that had apparently been dormant. She was flirting with him!

"I confess to the crime of *not* being The Neapolitan Nightingale! I further confess to having been no nearer to Naples, Italy than Naples, Florida, where I was born. I suppose it was that sliver of fact that allowed my creative spouse to create his edifice of publicity, until I almost believed it myself. I hope you won't think less of me—or you, Dr Watson . . ." (I am persuaded that the lady knew simple hero worship when she saw it.) And she gave a little mock bow.

"No matter where its owner hails from, madam," I said, returning the bow, "the voice came from the gods!"

At which point another voice joined our conversation. "Ah, my darling wife, collecting new admirers," it said. "Who was it who said you can remove the diva from the applause but never the applause from the diva? Mark Twain, I suspect."

"Quite possibly. It doesn't quite have the edge of our own Mr Wilde. But, unfortunately, at the moment neither does he." (Wilde at the time was languishing in Reading gaol.) "Florenz Adler, I presume?" And Holmes moved towards the stage, where the impresario stood in casually mannered pose, as if waiting for the inevitable photographer to appear with tripod and cloth.

He was an impressive figure, though it was not immediately obvious why this was so. He stood at no more than medium height and could not be described as conventionally handsome. Nonetheless, there was a suppressed power about him. The man was a life force and every moment of that life was etched on his face. It had the sculpted look that belonged on a marble bust or Roman coin. The expensive coat with its astrakhan collar draped casually over his shoulders was merely a theatrical prop which, frankly, the man didn't need. But my instinctive observation, which had gained something over the years from Holmes's tutoring, told me he thought he did. Florenz Adler would be a difficult and contrary man to deal with and he had timed his entrance to perfection, like the former actor we knew him to be.

His wife's reply surprised me. "No, my dear, I leave that to you." Was that an edge to her voice that I detected? "And now, gentlemen, if you will excuse me, I must go and supervise the costumes for tomorrow's rehearsals. As a performer the lesson one must learn is that, even though the curtain may have fallen, there is another world behind the scenes."

With that she was gone, retreating along the corridor that we had traversed earlier. Adler's eyes followed her but his expression was impossible to read. Then he turned on his considerable charm and beamed it in our direction. "Well, gentlemen, as you must know, your fame has long since o'erleaped the pond that divides us. So what brings the famous Sherlock Holmes and his equally famous colleague, Dr James H. Watson to grace my unworthy scaffold?"

Holmes's reaction to the question surprised me. He brushed aside the curtain of words and fixed Adler with the piercing gaze I knew so well. "Mr

Adler, neither of us believes your re-creation of Shakespeare's theatre to be anything but a magnificent feat of imagination . . . My congratulations to you and all those who have realised a dream so many have found to be impossible. That, however, is not why Dr Watson and I are here . . ."

"Mr Holmes," Adler interrupted, "forgive my earlier brusqueness. I have perhaps spent too much time among people whose instincts are to dramatise every emotion and to expect the same in return. My wife is always telling me that I cannot distinguish between my real feelings and what may create an immediate effect on others. I fear she may well be right but . . ." and here he laughed but without real amusement—"it will be a long time before I admit that to *her!* That little admission aside, let me say most sincerely that, whatever business brings you here, you are both most welcome."

"You might say that Mr Shakespeare brings us all here in one way or another but in our case the reason is less clear than your own. Perhaps you can help clarify it." And with that he produced the note we had been shown in Baker Street and handed it to Adler. Adler studied it carefully, turning it this way and that, his expression growing increasingly puzzled. If the man *was* acting, his performance, without benefit of rehearsal, was in a class of its own.

"I would surely like to, Mr Holmes," he said at length, betraying the first trace of an American accent I had so far noticed, "but you've got me baffled. What is this and where did it come from?"

"I was informed that it was delivered to you this very morning. My informant is your daughter, Flora. Do we have our facts wrong?"

"Just about as wrong as they get, Mr Holmes. I've never laid eyes on this piece of paper in my life but that's not the half of the problem we have here. The real problem is—I *have* no daughter. No Flora, no Fauna, no anything. I'm afraid Carlotta and I left all that too late, what with her career and one thing and another. I sometimes wish I'd had *three* daughters, then we could all have appeared together. I think I'd have made a pretty fair Lear. There are those who claim I have—without even setting foot on the stage! But tell me, Mr Holmes—what in Hades is going on here?"

If Holmes was surprised, he hid it behind his usual impassive demeanour. "In that case, Mr Adler, perhaps you'll be good enough to show me the other note you *did* receive this morning?"

"But Holmes," I interjected, "don't you remember he destroyed the earlier notes?" Then I remembered the source of that information and busied myself clearing a small cough that seemed to be developing.

Adler looked at my friend as I imagined he must have looked at many a performer auditioning for him. "What makes you think there *is* another note?"

"When a man's hand instinctively strays to his inside pocket before he can control his reactions, it is reasonable to assume that he carries something to which he attaches a degree of importance. When that reaction is triggered by the sight of an identical communication, the inference is virtually complete. May I see it, please? You thought it important enough not to destroy it but it may be much more significant—and yes, perhaps even dangerous—than you possibly imagine."

Adler hesitated only momentarily before putting his hand inside his jacket and removing another scrap of paper that looked to my eye well read. So the brash impresario was not as unconcerned as he might like us to believe.

"I see your reputation is well earned, Mr Holmes, and I must admit I would welcome having some light shed on the matter. Abuse I can handle and threats come cheap in my business. I guess there are a lot of people out there who would welcome my come-uppance, as they would call it. No, I'm pretty used to all that and I don't think I'm an easy man to scare but there's something real weird about this whole business. Somebody pretty smart is going to a lot of trouble. Or maybe it's because I'm superstitious enough not to take anything the Bard says lightly." He jumped down lightly from the stage and handed Holmes the note.

Once again there were two separate quotations. The first read:

LIKE ONE THAT DRAWS THE MODEL OF A HOUSE BEYOND HIS POWER TO BUILD IT
Henry IV (Pt.2)

While beneath it, as if in answer . . .

NOR BUILD THEIR EVILS ON THE GRAVES OF GREAT MEN.
Henry VIII

Holmes looked up from his perusal of the paper. "Whoever our friend is, he is working overtime on his *Concordance*. It has often been said that Shakespeare has an appropriate line for every occasion and now we are receiving proof of it."

If he had ever lost his composure, Florenz Adler now had it firmly back under control. Indicating that Holmes might keep the note, he said: "The thing that baffles me, Mr Holmes, is why *now?* I could understand this better if it had happened when I was first talking about doing this but the darned thing is almost finished, as you can see." He swept his arm around his head to indicate the structure that surrounded us. Not for the first time since we had entered did I have the sense that we were all of us somehow players on its stage and that this is where the final act of this drama—whatever it turned out to be—would be played out.

"Indeed," Holmes replied, "but the human mind works in complex ways. The dream to rebuild this particular playhouse, to re-create the cradle of theatre as we have come to know it, is one that has burned in many of them. For one reason or another none of those schemes came to pass. There are those who believe the Globe is not *destined* to be rebuilt. Perhaps our quoting friend is one of them. However, I believe it to be more likely that he has some reason to wish to frustrate your *personal* attempt and, if he cannot achieve that, to extract some form of revenge."

"So you think I really *am* in danger?"

"Perhaps. Were this confined to you alone, I might be inclined to dismiss it as the affectation of some jealous competitor but we have reason to believe that our curious correspondent has now cast his net wider to include certain others that we cannot afford to ignore. And last but not least, he has thrown down the gauntlet to Dr Watson and myself and I would be less than honest if I were not to admit that that aspect of the case intrigues me greatly. And since I know you have an appointment at Court, so to speak, a very few days from now, it behooves us to draw the threads together with all dispatch."

Adler looked at Holmes soberly for a moment:

"I put myself in your hands, Mr Holmes. Between now and opening night—or rather, afternoon—I'll take your advice implicitly. Just let's try and keep things to ourselves. OK? Actors in rehearsal can get pretty distracted. There's a lot at stake here for everyone—not least 'the bubble reputation'."

Hearing a sudden increase of noise behind him from the stage above, Adler turned his head. "Ah, right on cue. 'The players are come hither'. Gentlemen, join me on the stage and let me introduce you . . ."

As he led us round to where some temporary steps allowed us to climb up on to the stage without undue acrobatics, Adler pointed out some of the people who had been drifting onto it one or two at a time during the latter part of our subdued conversation.

"As I'm sure you know, the Globe was used mainly as a summer theatre. Your famous English weather saw to that even then. And while the Elizabethans may have ignored a drop of rain—you'll have noticed the wooden 'O' is somewhat open to the elements—I rather doubt that your fellow citizens would welcome a drenching today . . . Next season we shall be open in earnest from May but this year, after Her Majesty has done the honours, we shall content ourselves with a short 'Prologue Season' to get our players used to the space in which they must strut and fret."

"And on which one of the Bard's great works will you raise your curtain?" I asked, then quickly added—"Not that you have a curtain to raise, of course."

"Not on any one, doctor," Adler answered. "We thought the Queen should be allowed to dine from a menu of Shakespeare's best. Consequently, we shall perform a series of scenes from different plays. That way we can not only exploit this unique stage, but also what we hope will be the equally unique talents of the actors we have assembled."

"Over there, for instance, is Hamilton Fiske . . ." He indicated a large florid man who was circling one of the stage pillars, muttering to himself. He was bent over in an uncomfortable position that reminded me irresistibly of the Hunchback of Notre Dame. "He played with Irving, you know," Adler explained. "And if you don't know, he'll soon tell you. Actually, I believe he understudied the Fool to Irving's Lear five or six years ago and he's been playing the fool ever since. I'm afraid he and Bacchus are excessively close friends but he is a beloved figure of West End audiences and so . . ."

"I assume we are watching an embryonic Richard III taking shape?" said Holmes.

"Indeed. Hamilton says he's determined to find new meaning in 'My kingdom for a horse,' and he's been going around with that pillow in the back of his shirt for days, so that he can 'feel' the hump. He says he's developing his own 'method' and I can tell you it's one hell of a job trying to direct someone who keeps asking you for deeper 'meaning'. Heaven help us if all young actors start to worry about this 'method' nonsense."

Adler led us up to a group who were talking quietly together. Easily the most striking figure was an elderly lady, ramrod straight with elegantly coifed silver hair. Before Adler could introduce her, Holmes gave a small bow and addressed her: "It has long been my ambition to meet the Grand Dame of the English theatre. Watson, come and be introduced to Dame Ivy Fosdyke . . ."

I found myself looking into the most piercing blue eyes I can ever recall and it was clear from the expression in them that the lady was not impervious to his flattery. I can still remember her younger self on picture postcards and she had been a famous beauty in her day, courted by various members of the nobility, although for some reason she had never married any of them. "*Enchanté*, Dr Watson. I am an avid reader of your narratives." And she held out the tips of her fingers for me to touch.

"I do implore you to take Watson's 'narratives' with the proverbial pinch of salt," Holmes smiled. "Tell him that if he is not careful, he will soon rival the excesses of Mrs Radcliffe! I believe Shakespeare is a new departure for you, Dame

Ivy? I always associate you with more domestic pieces."

"To be sure, Mr Holmes, no one has ever poured a more elegant cup of tea than Dame Ivy on the Broadway or West End stage." The interjection came from Carlotta Adler, who had now joined the group, carrying some material draped over one arm.

"Too kind, my dear," said the Dame with a slightly forced smile. "Coming from you, I must take that as a compliment. No, Mr Holmes, my days of pouring tea are over. My Muse has beckoned me to higher things. I hope to be able to show Her Majesty the softer side of Juliet's Nurse, for instance." Then, turning to Carlotta, "I see you have the fabrics I asked for. Perhaps we should go and try them. I know you must have so many little chores to attend to." Taking Carlotta firmly by the arm, she graced us all with an angelic smile and retreated upstage. It may have been my imagination but the temperature seemed to rise immediately.

"I suppose we should be grateful for small mercies." It was Adler speaking so that only Holmes and I could hear. "It's taken me years to get her to act her age. The woman insisted on playing Juliet until she was well into her fifties!" I thought I saw a fleeting expression cross my friend's face and, had we had a moment for a private word, things might have turned out very differently. As it was, we were distracted by another voice.

"Aren't you going to introduce me, Flo? I know it's age before beauty, so now it's my turn." The speaker was a strikingly pretty young woman in her late 20s and her portrait was all over the popular papers at the time. Pauline French had been a famous Gaiety Girl until she'd turned actress a year or so ago. In fact, now I came to think of it, several writers had compared her to Ivy Fosdyke in her heyday—a comparison which can hardly have pleased the older woman.

"Forgive me, my dear." It seemed to me that Adler was showing her undue deference and I couldn't help thinking back to Carlotta's earlier remark. A man in Adler's position must always be surrounded by attractive young women. "Gentlemen, our Juliet, our Ophelia . . . our Cleopatra, Miss Pauline French."

"Hey, come on, Mr Adler. Ladies first is fine with me but we can't let them upstage us entirely." A fresh-faced young man stepped forward and thrust out a hand for Holmes to shake. "Harrison Trent, Mr Holmes. And may I say I'm one of your greatest fans? Have been ever since *The Sign of Four*. And, of course, yours, too, Dr Watson," he added hastily.

Adler stepped forward and put an arm around the young man's shoulders. "It doesn't take a Sherlock Holmes to detect yet another American

53

accent. I've always wanted ours to be an international company, so I'm starting as I mean to go on. Harrison is a fine young actor, just beginning to make a name for himself over the other side. I know I'm being totally objective when I say that, even though his father was one of my oldest friends and associates. Harry will be giving us his Brutus, Horatio and, not least, his Antony."

Looking at Trent, I could more easily picture that stocky frame riding the range or chopping down trees than wearing a toga but then, Holmes is always accusing me of being a conservative in these matters. To my mind the true Shakespearean actor should have the aquiline features and the chiseled nose of a Henry Irving. He should look more like—well, more like Holmes, I suppose. And, to be fair, the next young man Adler brought forward did.

"Gentlemen, may I introduce Ted Allan." I put Allan—like Trent—as being somewhere in his early thirties but he was a good six inches taller and, whereas the former had a ruddy outdoor complexion, his appearance provided a dramatic contrast with a shock of black hair offset by a pale, unlined face. This young man had every chance of becoming what I believe is known as a "matinée idol". When he spoke the voice was resonant and I couldn't help feeling that he had practised hard to make it so. He was totally aware of the impression he created.

"Mr Holmes, I might as well confess right away. I, too, share the same passport as Mr Adler and my colleague here. My only defence is my conviction that your compatriot, whose work we are here to celebrate, wrote not merely for the people of this scept'red isle but for mankind. I rest my case . . ." And he gave a small mock bow. It was done as elegantly and mellifluously as if it had been rehearsed and I wasn't quite sure why it hadn't moved me more. Perhaps because it was *too* perfect.

"In this case I plead not guilty, Mr Holmes," Adler threw up his hands in mock horror. "I didn't smuggle Ted into the country. He turned up at my hotel, auditioned for me without letting me get a word in edgewise and, knowing talent when I see it, I hired him on the spot. He'll be our Cassius and our Hamlet."

"Well, Mr Adler, if he learns his *Hamlet* as well as he knows his *Richard II*, I'm sure he'll do very well," said Holmes.

"*Richard II*? We're not doing *Richard II* . . ." Adler sounded puzzled and didn't I notice Allan's smile momentarily freeze?

"I was referring to John of Gaunt's speech in the play from which Mr Allan was quoting just now—

This royal throne of kings, this scept'red isle,
This earth of majesty, this seat of Mars,

This other Eden, demiparadise,
This fortress built by Nature for herself
Against infection and the hand of war,
This happy breed of men, this little world,
This precious stone set in the silver sea,
Which serves it in the office of a wall
Or as a moat defensive to a house
Against the envy of less happier lands;
This blessed plot, this earth, this realm . . ."

He paused briefly before concluding—"this *England.*" I swear you could have heard the proverbial pin drop. Then Adler spoke, looking at my friend, as it seemed to me with even greater respect. "Mr Holmes, if you ever want a job . . ."

"Thank you, Mr Adler, but I acquired one earlier this morning and I'm afraid Watson and I must be about that business. But it would be rude of us to take our leave without meeting this gentleman . . ." And here he turned to the last member of the group, who had just hurried on to the stage rather out of breath.

A foppish young man—perhaps a year or two younger than Trent or Allan—he stepped forward with an exaggerated bow. Instead of the casual rehearsal clothes of the others, he was immaculately attired in houndstooth check trousers, a black velvet jacket, silk cravat and in his buttonhole—a green carnation, rather obviously dyed, since to the best of my knowledge Mother Nature does not include the colour in her palette for carnations.

"Simon Phipps at your service, gentlemen. It is just possible, I suppose, that you may have seen me in Oscar Wilde's *The Importance of Being Earnest*. I understudied Algernon and was privileged to appear three times. Such friends of mine who missed those three occasions consider themselves the fortunate ones! Alas, poor Oscar, to find himself in durance vile for practices the common Roman or Greek considered commonplace . . ."

The soliloquy might well have continued indefinitely, had Adler not interrupted, as I suspect he had to do quite often. "What Simon would never tell you, if he were to take all night—which he is perfectly capable of doing—is that he was the youngest actor ever to graduate from the Royal Academy of Dramatic Art and would undoubtedly have bestrode the British boards like a colossus, had he not listened to the siren song and gone off, like Columbus, to discover America. Luckily for us, the song ended and he returned."

"Ah," said Phipps, removing a pristine handkerchief from his sleeve and striking a self-mocking pose, "I'm inclined to believe that America never has been discovered. I myself would say that it had merely been detected. The Master—from *The*

Picture of Dorian Gray." And he bowed to the assembled company.

"And there, Mr Holmes, Dr Watson," Adler concluded with a tight little smile, "you have the principals of our little company. Of course, we also have a number of spear carriers."

"Of whom I consider myself one, although this time I come bearing gifts not spears." We turned to find Carlotta Adler bearing down on the group, her arms almost filled with an enormous bouquet of red roses. "I do hope this is not going to become a habit. I hate flowers when they're not for me." She smiled but there was little genuine humour in it. In my mind's eye I could see her once again smiling and bowing on that long ago concert platform as the flowers came and came . . .

"The lady doth protest too much, methinks." It was Fiske joining the group and wiping away the signs of his recent exertions with a large towel. "For women are as roses . . ."

But it was Allan who took up the line—
" '. . . whose fair flower being once display'd doth fall that very hour.' *Twelfth Night.* Not a particularly appropriate thought under the circumstances, Ham, if I may say so. But they really are beautiful. Who are they for, Carlotta?"

"They were left at the stage door with a note with Pauline's name on it. I thought I'd bring them over. Here you are, my dear."

As she handed the bouquet to the obviously pleased Miss French, a small piece of white paper fluttered to the stage. Awkwardly clutching the outsize bunch of roses, the young actress tried to bend to pick it up. At which moment Holmes did a most extraordinary thing. He stepped close to her and struck the flowers out of her grasp. "Everyone stand back!" he said in a voice that brooked no argument. "Ah, as I thought."

From among the scattered flowers slithered a small green snake.

Allan was the first to react. Stepping forward, he brought his boot down with great force, breaking its back. A moment later Holmes was on his knees by the corpse. "Careful, Holmes," I cried, "it might not be dead."

"Oh, it's dead, right enough," Holmes said, quietly examining the remains. "*Coluber*, the common or garden grass snake. Be kind enough to read the note that accompanied it, will you? Watson. If it doesn't say . . .

YOU SPOTTED SNAKES WITH DOUBLE TONGUE

"I miss my guess. *A Midsummer Night's Dream*," he added in elucidation. I snatched up the paper and glanced at it quickly. "You're absolutely right. But how did you . . . ?"

Holmes rose to his feet. "I'm afraid our

correspondent is beginning to cut corners. A pity—I had expected more of a challenge. As you see, no spots and the tongue, such as it is, has been removed. This poor little chap could not possibly have done anyone any harm, unless he happened to *frighten* you to death, Miss French."

"But why *me?*" Pauline French was still shaking in the protective arm of Carlotta Adler.

"Who else but Cleopatra would be the recipient of an asp? And since asps are fortunately in short supply, this is some sort of approximation, courtesy of any competent pet shop." Then he turned to the group, all of whom were just beginning to recover their composure. "Ladies and gentlemen, I can well imagine that this little episode must be somewhat confusing for you. Unfortunately, I must leave Mr Adler to give you the general details of the situation we now face, as he thinks fit. Mr Adler, with your permission Dr Watson and I will return tomorrow, when I believe you will be rehearsing. Until then, goodbye to you all—and particularly to our American cousins.

"As Watson will tell you, I have long believed that the myopia of a long dead monarch and the subsequent shortsightedness of certain Ministers of State have merely postponed the cultural merging of two great nations that share so much— even if their language often seems to be a questionable part of it. No, Mr Phipps, *not* Mr Wilde—Mr Holmes . . ."

With that he raised his hat to the ladies, took me by the arm and steered me towards the exit. I barely had time to raise my own hat and we were in the tunnel and out of their sight.

CHAPTER FOUR

As we sat in the cab on our way back to Baker Street, I asked, "Well, Holmes, what do you make of it?" Gazing out of the window Holmes paused for a moment:

"I have always believed it to be a mistake to come to a conclusion before one has all the evidence, and we are far from having all the evidence in this case. Nonetheless, certain facts do present themselves which suggest avenues of exploration. But come, Watson, you know my methods—apply them. What have *you* observed?"

"My money's on that Phipps fellow," I said firmly. "You noticed how he came in later than the others? He could be our paperboy. Rushes back, leaves the flowers at the stage door, joins the group, so as to be there when they're delivered. Probably in with that Carlotta woman. She's obviously jealous of the younger woman with her husband. On the other hand, where was Fiske when we were talking to the others? He made a big play to catch our attention when we first arrived. Could have slunk off when we weren't looking. Or Dame Ivy, come to think of it, when she went off with Carlotta. But no, I think you'll find Phipps is mixed up in it. Chap that dresses like that. And I'll swear he was wearing perfume . . ."

"*Eau de toilette*, to be fair, old fellow. What the well dressed man about town is wearing, if he wishes to be noticed and Master Simon certainly wishes to create a certain impression. Yes, he may very well have some part to play in this little drama as well as the ones penned by Mr Shakespeare. So, indeed, may several of them. The American connection is too strong to be coincidental. Hence my remark about the 'American Cousins'. Let them worry that we are on the scent. As for your other observations, Watson, I fear you were distracted, as you were meant to be, from the significant facts."

"Which were?"

"Before we come to them, let me dispose of the others. There is nothing effeminate about young Phipps. For reasons best known to himself, he merely wishes to appear so. The reason he was late making his entrance was because, having seen us arrive, he was putting the last touches to his costume. He was dyeing his carnation. It was still wet when he arrived. Indeed, he had traces of green on his fingers, which he took care to wipe before he shook hands. Nor do I believe there was collusion between him and Carlotta. Women have a notorious aversion to snakes and I know of none who would be able to carry a bouquet of flowers as casually as Mrs Adler did, knowing that they contained. And, by the way, Phipps shares her feelings. When he saw the snake, his complexion was a good match for his *boutonnière*!"

"But what was the purpose of the snake?"

"Purely to gain attention. Our friend is telling us to take him seriously. He wants to achieve his ends without having to go too far but he is reminding us that he could just as easily have introduced something more deadly. He may even be deliberately playing with metaphors. A snake—in the grass or out of it—can hardly be considered a compliment and 'double tongue' underlines the hypocrisy he clearly feels Adler and his followers are guilty of. He is beginning to show an interesting turn of mind, whoever he is. We are sailing into deeper waters and we need to know more about our fellow passengers. By the way, Watson, did it not strike you as strange that none of them asked us why we were there? Some of them, at least, were expecting us."

"Was there anything else of consequence that I failed to observe?" I asked as the cab turned into Baker Street.

"Nothing beyond the fact that Dame Ivy was our early morning visitor. Her handshake is as distinctive a signature as her perfume. Why do women take so much trouble with the surface trappings and forget the little things which are infinitely the most important. Whoever is master-minding this affair has gone to some considerable pains to involve me. They have done their homework. And yet they have overlooked my ability to distinguish between seventy-five different perfumes, despite the fact that I have published a paper on the subject. So we know *who* impersonated Flora Adler—and to take off thirty years, even with the benefit of gloves and veil, betokens a considerable actress, I think you'll agree. But then, a fifty year old Juliet *is* a considerable actress by definition. You see now, Watson, why she could not take off her gloves? Her hands would have given her away immediately. The hands and the neck are the first places to show a woman's age.

"What we have yet to learn is—*why?* Why go to all this trouble? Why invent a character in 'Flora Adler' who is certain to be discovered with the first question I ask her 'father'?"

"Because their homework has told them that it is the theatricality of circumstance that invariably tempts you to accept a case," I suggested, then added modestly, "an aspect I flatter myself I have occasionally been able to convey to some degree."

"Precisely, Watson, precisely. By now it *is* a piece of theatre that has been devised. It is no longer enough to have Adler pack up his tents and silently steal away. He must be forced to do so publicly and see himself humiliated in the process. They are setting the stage—whoever *they* are—and they are succeeding. We shall see the play out. But there is one other problem that is concerning me, another gap I intend to fill forthwith . . ."

"And that is?"

"It may have escaped your attention, Watson, that we have eaten nothing since your interrupted breakfast. I suggest a small supper at Rule's and then perhaps we might look into one of your music halls. I believe we have had quite enough culture for one day."

When I came down to breakfast the next morning, I found Holmes sitting in his usual chair examining a somewhat grubby piece of paper. As if in answer to my unspoken question, he passed it across to me.

"It appears that we had a visitor while we were out on the town, Watson. Mr Hamilton Fiske apparently graced us with his theatrical presence, according to Mrs Hudson. She described him as being 'very excitable' and rather upset to find that we were out. He left the note you have in your hand."

The "note" was, in fact, Fiske's business card and it appeared to have had rather hard wear. Following Holmes's practice, I should have deduced that his career was not in a particularly successful phase and that the gentleman was an inveterate snuff taker. I turned my attention to the contents of the card.

E. HAMILTON FISKE
Thespian Extraordinary

. . . said the front face, while on the reverse in a flamboyant and rather unsteady hand . . .

"I may know something of our quaint Quoter. Will call on you tomorrow early."

At that moment there was the ring of the door-bell. "And that may well be the very gentleman now," said Holmes, arranging the cord of his old dressing gown to receive his visitor.

Instead, Mrs Hudson ushered in the familiar figure of Inspector Lestrade. Small, rather under average height, he had a face that had given me occasion to think more than once over the years that resembled the hunted rather than the hunter. Nonetheless, in his own plodding way he had often been useful to Holmes who, I knew, had a fondness for the man and had passed on the credit for solving many a case, when he preferred to avoid the attendant publicity.

Since he was practically a member of the family, so to speak, it never occurred to me to edit my speech. Handing the card back to Holmes, as Lestrade was in the very act of removing his hat, I said something to the effect of Fiske's card being safer in Holmes's keeping and my being notorious for mislaying things. If I had wished to stop someone in their tracks, I could not have devised a better stratagem.

"Did you say 'Fiske', Doctor? Oh, good

morning, gentlemen. Forgive my early intrusion. Not *Hamilton* Fiske, the *actor?*"

"Well, yes, as a matter of fact," I said a little huffily. It was by no means the first time he had cut across one of my conversations with my friend and without making an issue of it, I wanted to make the point that we were used to certain standards of social behaviour.

"Why do you ask, Lestrade?" Holmes was now leaning forward in his chair, completely focused on our visitor.

"Because I'm on my way to see him, Mr Holmes. I just dropped in on my way to bring you these . . ." And he handed Holmes a sheaf of papers. "They're some of the answers to the telegrams you asked us to send out last night. Not that I've read them," he added hastily. "Your boy, Billy, said you'd want to see them as soon as they came in, so I thought I'd drop them in myself. Always happy to return a favour."

"I'm most grateful to you, Lestrade. But might I ask where you are going to see Fiske? We were rather expecting a visit from that gentleman ourselves."

"In that case, I'm afraid you're in for a long wait, Mr Holmes," Lestrade replied, rather pleased for once, it seemed to me, to be in a position to tell Sherlock Holmes something he did not already know. "Just as I was leaving the Yard we got word that his body had been found under rather peculiar circumstances not too far from here in Marsham Square. I've given instructions for the area to be cordoned off until my men and I get there."

"Under the circumstances you won't mind if Watson and I join you?" said Holmes, swiftly exchanging his dressing gown for a jacket. It was more a statement than a question and Lestrade took it as such. "It's just possible that we may be able to be of assistance to each other. Not . . ." and he inclined his head towards the Inspector—"for the first time, as I recall. I imagine you have your vehicle waiting outside . . . ?"

A few minutes later we found ourselves alighting in a rundown square somewhere in the back of Islington. It was an area I had never had occasion to frequent in either my personal or professional capacity and nothing about it suggested that I had missed a great deal. It spoke of lives lived on the edge of poverty but more than that, it suggested a poverty of hope. Some of the houses were boarded up with windows that looked like nothing so much as missing teeth. And yet the elegance of the architecture indicated a more affluent past. It was altogether a depressing picture as the early morning sun struggled to make its presence felt.

Two uniformed constables greeted Lestrade deferentially and one of them clearly recognised Holmes, for he blurted out—"Morning, Mr Holmes. You remember me, sir? Baker? I was with you and the Doctor in that Coburg Square bank business with the red-headed fellows. We'll soon have this sorted out now that *you're* here." If he had been about to say anything further, a glance from Lestrade changed his mind. Instead he led us over to the centre of the square, where several other policemen were gathered.

The main feature of Marsham Square—and its original pride, I have no doubt—was an impressive equestrian statue of some long forgotten statesman. "It has always been my conviction that fully half the men who grace a sculpted steed would lose their seats within seconds were the horse flesh and blood," Holmes murmured to me as we approached it. It was then that I noticed something the sculptor had hardly intended. Behind the rider whose outstretched arm pointed to far horizons another figure was seated, its arms around the stone figure. The second man had his face turned in our direction and the strengthening light was good enough for me to recognise the florid features of the man we had seen on the Globe stage the previous day. Then the expression had been animated but now it was frozen in the rictus of a dead smile. My immediate impression, a quite unworthy one, I confess, was of an actor playing the part of a corpse.

Then Holmes interrupted my reverie. "So Richard found his horse but it cost him his kingdom, I fear."

"*Richard?*" It was a puzzled Lestrade. "I

thought his name was *Hamilton*. Edward Hamilton Fiske, according to our files."

"You're quite right, of course, Lestrade," Holmes replied. "It was something Watson and I were discussing earlier. Pray continue."

Lestrade consulted a paper handed to him by a uniformed sergeant. "It seems young Baker here was going though the square on his normal rounds in the early hours when he happened to shine his lamp up to check the upper windows. We get a lot of vandalism in these back streets, though why they bother beats me. Well, you might as well tell us in your own words, Baker. Just don't make a meal of it."

"Right, sir," said the young constable, addressing himself to Holmes. "I don't shine the light up on every round, so I might have missed him the previous time. But when I *did* see him— must have been around . . ."

"Four-thirty, should have been." This from Lestrade, consulting the sergeant's notes.

"That's right. Four-thirty. I blew me whistle for help. And do you know, I had the strangest feeling somebody was watching me from the shadows but, if they were, the noise must have frightened off whoever it was. Then, while I was waiting, I shone the lamp around and looked very care-fully—just like I seen Mr Holmes do that time— being careful not to interfere with any clues there might be." He looked at Holmes for approval.

"You did quite right, Baker—didn't he, Lestrade?" said Holmes. "Now, let's see what else the statue has to tell us." And with that he began to circle it like a dog on the scent. It was Holmes as I had seen him so often, his brows drawn in lines that could have been etched and the eyes beneath them gleaming fiercely with the concentration he summoned up. He walked around twice, first clockwise, then anti-clockwise, finally dropping to his knees and examining a particular patch of earth with the powerful lens he always carried. At length, he seemed satisfied. Rising to his feet he dusted his knees, rolling a little of the dirt between his long fingers.

"Very well, Lestrade, perhaps you will ask your men to bring down the body? I'd be obliged if you would allow Dr Watson to make a preliminary examination before the coroner performs the usual post mortem."

As one constable was given a leg up by his colleagues, he was able to dislodge Fiske's body. Reluctantly, it seemed, the actor gave up his embrace of the unknown rider and was lowered to the ground, where he was placed on a waiting sheet.

"As you see, gentlemen," said Holmes, while this procedure was taking place, "this was the work of two men. Even with his co-operation in life, Fiske was too heavy for one man to lift him in place. There is ample confirmation in the footprints around the base of the statue. Two men approached it, supporting a third who was altogether larger. Although the latter's feet were dragging, he appears to have had some means of locomotion. Then there are clear signs of scuffing and two sets of deeper footprints, as they heave him into position. Finally, they depart. Interestingly, one of them at a run—perhaps losing his nerve—while the other's return tread is more measured. The body's weight kept it in position— and I would venture a guess that Mr Fiske made his final exit, leaving us his too, too solid flesh, while he was actually in the saddle. Oh, and he left us one more thing . . ."

And Holmes handed me a small glass capsule half full of a clear liquid. "This almost certainly fell from Fiske's pocket as the body settled." As I took it gingerly, Lestrade—feeling that it was time he made some contribution to the proceedings— interjected: "But how do we know it was anything to do with Fiske? How do we know it hadn't been there for days?"

"Because this is normally a busy square and something as obvious would certainly be picked up, if it were not first trodden under foot. Second, the outside of the capsule is dry, yet the ground and the footprints are damp. I believe it rained slightly in the early hours, did it not, Baker?"

"Indeed it did, sir."

"At which point," Holmes continued, "I deduce

the body shifted due to rigor mortis, dislodging the evidence. You've found something, Watson?"

While Holmes was talking, I had been giving the body a cursory examination. Dead about four hours, it appeared, taking the warm night air into account. No apparent signs of violence. From the man's general appearance and what little I knew of his way of life, I would have been inclined to suspect a heart attack. Searching through his pockets I found a small card, which made interesting reading. It was this which caught my friend's eye and I handed it to him. He read the small print that was the password to many a man's life or death.

"So, our friend was a diabetic. And this, I assume"—indicating the capsule—"the injection of insulin that he should have taken, had he not been otherwise occupied."

Before Lestrade could stop him, Holmes had unscrewed the capsule, taken a drop on the tip of his finger and tasted it. "As I thought."

"Seems pretty cut and dried, then, Mr Holmes," said Lestrade, trying to reassert a degree of authority. "These three fellows go out on a bit of a spree—you see, Doctor, I *did* notice the smell of alcohol as they brought him down. One thing leads to another and for a lark he decides he wants to get up on his high horse, so to speak. The other two help him up, he comes over queer, they lose their nerve and make a run for it. Don't you think so, Mr Holmes?"

"As ever, Lestrade, you have a few of the facts but little of the truth. As to what Fiske drank or what was *in* the drink we shall have to wait until the results of the post mortem but I doubt that a simple excess of alcohol will prove to be the answer. I'm afraid that lies here . . ." And leaning over the corpse, Holmes removed the small white rose that adorned its buttonhole.

"Good heavens, old fellow, how did I come to miss that?" I apologised.

"Because you were looking where any trained medical man is bound to look—at the body in question," Holmes replied. "Ah, yes, here we are." His fingers had been searching Fiske's clothes with a brisk thoroughness and now from an inside pocket he produced a familiar piece of folded white paper. I stood up and read it over his shoulder.

AN TWO MEN RIDE OF A HORSE, ONE MUST RIDE BEHIND
Much Ado About Nothing

"A great deal of ado, I fear, and about something which has now taken the irrevocable step over the edge of the abyss. I had hoped our literary friend would be content to play his conundrums but it seems his plans have taken a more lethal turn. Due, I have little doubt, to this gentleman's involvement in the plot." And he indicated Fiske's body, which the policemen were now busy covering with a sheet.

"Will someone *please* tell me what's going on?" Lestrade pleaded, leading us towards his cab. And on the journey back to Baker Street Holmes did give him an edited version of events . . .

CHAPTER FIVE

We were in our sitting room and Lestrade was on his way back to Scotland Yard and the inevitable paperwork attendant on sudden death: "Come, Watson, I know your moods well enough, I think, after all these years. You think I confided too much in our friend, Lestrade?"

"Well," I replied, "since you ask, I *was* rather surprised you were so forthcoming, since you know who is involved." I hesitated to be more specific even in the privacy of our own room. And, to be fair to Holmes, the name had not passed his lips in briefing Lestrade.

"I must confess that, had he not been so embroiled already, I might have been a little more reticent. As it is, I have no wish to see the official bloodhounds blundering about and confusing what promises to be a most interesting scent. They have their limitations, to be sure, as we have seen more than once in the past, but the thoroughness of the British policeman is without parallel. I have no wish to see them off the leash. On the contrary, we must harness them to our purpose. Fiske's murder means that time is running out."

"Murder? What makes you so sure it was *murder?*" I replied. "Why couldn't it have been a drunken spree? Fellow has a heart attack and the other two panic and leave him. Oh, no, that doesn't explain the note and the rose—unless it was another warning that got out of hand . . . ?"

"Nor does it explain the capsule."

"You mean the insulin?"

"Except it *wasn't* insulin."

"But you said . . ." I objected.

"I said it was as I thought," Holmes interrupted. "The capsule contained nothing more than good old London tap water. You may have observed that I put it in my pocket. No need to confuse Lestrade further. No, Watson, this was murder just as much as if he'd swallowed poison. Murder by omission if not by commission. A diabetic needs his needle regularly. I think you will grant I have some personal knowledge of that particular experience? To be deprived of it . . . but we must await the results of the post mortem which Lestrade—now our partner in this crime—will bring us post haste.

"Which reminds me, we have yet to see what news he brought us earlier." And with that he snatched up the sheaf of papers he had set on the table when we left with Lestrade and began to peruse them attentively. What he read seemed to satisfy him, for he passed one of the sheets over to me. "This begins to disperse the mist from the American connection, I fancy. What strikes you, Watson?"

The sheet was a cast list from a theatre

programme. Ford's Theatre, Washington. April 1865. *Our American Cousin.* That much we already knew. Florenz Adler in a supporting part. That we also knew. But "Miss Ivy Fosdyke"? That we certainly didn't know, and here was another familiar name . . . "Addison Trent". I must have been speaking my discoveries aloud, much to Holmes's amusement.

"Quite right, Watson. A few of the pieces do seem to be falling into place. The Chicago police have been kind enough to provide me with a little background commentary"—he flourished some of the other pages he'd been reading—"and it would appear that Dame Ivy—or should I say 'Miss Ivy'?—was not always the pillar of society, or indeed propriety, that we know today. The local rumour at the time was that she may have been engaged in a liaison with Adler, who happened to be married at the time to a lady in New York but, more interestingly, there was a scandal about some poison pen letters the leading lady was receiving and which our Miss Fosdyke was suspected of sending. The President's death obviously disrupted normal processes and the company disbanded. Now, all of this was a very long time ago but one cannot help but feel that the lady who has since become a revered figure of the English stage would hardly welcome the thought that some of those suppositions might be aired all over again. Do I not detect a whiff of brimstone and blackmail in the air—enough for someone to persuade the good lady to play a part in an alternative drama?"

"Yes, and what about this other fellow—*Trent?* Is he any relation?"

"The father of the young man we met yesterday. Quite right, Watson. Addison Trent. Like Adler, he appears to have lost the taste for appearing on the boards after this traumatic experience and also turned to promoting plays. You remember Adler spoke of him as being one of his oldest friends and associates? Well, it appears that Trent was also a significant competitor to Adler for quite a while, then suddenly went out of business. He apparently committed suicide a few years ago. That's all they were able to discover in the time but they'll keep on looking. This is a rich vein, Watson, and I sense we have merely scratched its surface."

"That's all very well, Holmes," I interjected, "but where does Fiske fit into all this. Surely he wasn't in this play, too?"

"No, I fancy not. I think we'll find his involvement is more recent and, unfortunately for him, somewhat short-lived. And now, old friend, if you'll excuse me, I have a few matters to attend to before we return to the Globe. If we should be a little later than our stated time, I feel sure they have enough to occupy them in the light of this morning's events. Let us rendezvous here at two, if that would be convenient."

Used as I was to Holmes's sudden mood swings, I muttered something about needing to drop in and make sure the practice was under control or something such and, instead, set off for a leisurely stroll through Regent's Park, while I tried to make some sense of recent happenings.

Somebody was intent on stopping an American impresario from building the replica of an Elizabethan theatre, to the point of threatening not only him and many of those closest to him but even the head of state. What was so special about *this* theatre? And what *was* the American connection? That seemed to explain Dame Ivy's involvement but who were the two men who made up "we three"? And what had Fiske known that made him so dangerous? Not for the first time I felt frustrated that I had nothing concrete to offer Holmes. Yet I was left with the feeling that some time in the last twenty-four hours one of the characters in this play had said something that should have given me a clue.

At which point the excuse I'd used about my practice actually did obtrude on my conscience. I hailed a cab and for the next hour or two occupied my mind with mundane matters like prescriptions and paperwork.

Little better off, except for the physical exercise, I returned to Baker Street where, to my surprise I found a strange and rather rotund man sitting in Holmes's usual chair. He had an unfashionably high collar and a high colour to go with it, which spoke of regular bouts with the bottle. Hair grew in tufts around the side of a shining bald pate but his most noticeable feature was a pair of bushy black eyebrows that perched there like caterpillars. When I asked him what he thought he was doing there, he replied in a voice clearly the worse for whisky that "Mr 'Olmes said as I should make meself comfortable and wait. He said this Watson feller would see me right."

"Right?" I said, my temper rising rapidly. "I'm 'this Watson feller', as you call him, and I'll see you right out of the door, my good man! I've never known such infernal cheek, sitting there as large as life, why . . ."

"Good old Watson," said the voice of Sherlock Holmes, "I can always rely on you to guard my back or, in this case, my front as well. I declare you have the instincts of the British bulldog crossed with the Stag at Bay!" So saying, the rotund gentleman proceeded to peel off his bushy eyebrows, take the padding from inside his cheeks and use a none-too-clean kerchief to wipe off what I could now see was makeup from his face. Soon the features of a cheery imbiber was replaced by the infinitely more saturnine countenance of my friend.

"Forgive me but you know my fondness for assuming other identities. It has always been my conviction that one of the primary skills of someone in my profession is the ability to see through a disguise, which is why I take such trouble with my own. I feel it helps me to occupy temporarily the mind of an opponent." He settled back comfortably, a sign that he had information to impart and a mind to do so.

"I was rather pleased with this new persona; in fact, I may use it again. The idea came into my mind, I must confess, when we saw Mr George Robey last night at the Oxford Music Hall. Not that I intend to attempt a comic song, Watson—you may set your mind at rest on that score! No, there is something about a cheerful looking man that softens people in their reaction to him. You will confide in such a man, particularly in the setting of a hostelry. Which is where I have spent my time since I saw you last. Several hostelries, in fact."

"Ah well," I muttered, somewhat mollified, "at least it isn't that filthy lascar you seem to inhabit so often. I suppose we should be grateful for small mercies."

Holmes continued as if I hadn't spoken. "I followed the trail of last evenings's revellers and quite a trail it turned out to be. If I may piece together a variety of accounts derived from several different publicans in the Islington area, Fiske seems to have repaired direct from his abortive visit to Baker Street to his habitual haunt, The Barley Mow in Islington High Street. The landlord there professed him to be in high spirits, to the point where he was ordering whisky instead of his usual port. His ship was about to come in, he kept saying, which somewhat confused mine host, since he said he'd 'always had him down as one of those actor fellers.'

"Later in the evening Fiske was apparently joined by a younger man he seemed to recognise, although by this time he was becoming rather maudlin and repetitive about his 'ship'. According to the landlord—whose memory suddenly became remarkably retentive after a further pint of his own watery ale—Fiske seemed puzzled by something about his friend's appearance. At one point he tried to tug the man's beard and asked him why he was wearing it."

"A false beard, I shouldn't wonder," I interjected. "Wanted to make sure no one could describe him later."

"Thank you, Watson. That possibility had indeed occurred to me also," Holmes smiled. "At which point the younger man paid their bill and hurried Fiske out. They were later seen at three other saloon bars with Fiske becoming steadily more inebriated. At the last—an insalubrious spot called The Frog and Parrot just one street away from Marsham Square—they were joined by a second young man, who arrived somewhat out of breath. His friend took him to task for being late and then became extremely agitated about the jacket the young man was wearing."

"The jacket?"

"It appears he was sporting a flower in his button hole. A green carnation."

"Phipps!"

"So it would appear. In any event, Gentlemen A tore the flower off and ground it underfoot. Soon after that he was heard to say—'I think he could do with a little help.' At which point he took a small syringe from Fiske's pocket and handed it to the second man, together with a small glass capsule that he took from his own pocket. By this time Fiske was absent except corporeally and raised no objection when he was led out by the newcomer, leaving the bearded man to pay for the drinks. That was the last time they were seen— until this morning."

Holmes settled himself into his chair and reached for a favourite pipe, so I knew there was more to come.

"My last port of call was Fiske's lodging house. I had managed to glean the address from the first landlord. Assuming that the news would not yet have reached there, I posed as an acting colleague, sent by my forgetful friend to pick up a spare hat. The landlady was perfectly affable—if you make a living dealing with 'rude theatricals', I imagine a certain *sangfroid* is obligatory. She showed some surprise, however, that the 'other young man' didn't pick it up when he was here earlier. Yes, Watson, I'm afraid we remain one step behind. It would appear that, while we were examining the remains of Mr Fiske, our literary friend was going through his possessions."

"What do you imagine he was looking for?" I interjected.

"Oh, some sort of note, almost certainly," Holmes replied, filling his old clay pipe ominously. "Something took place at the Globe yesterday after we left. Fiske saw or heard something that aroused his suspicions, presumably after Adler had given them some kind of explanation of events to date. Probably he saw the 'three' conferring. Not being the subtlest of men, his behaviour must have alerted them. One of them may have followed him when he paid us his abortive visit. Mrs Hudson now remembers a second caller, a young man with a scarf around his face, which he attributed to neuralgia. He rang the bell shortly after Fiske's departure, asking if Mr Sherlock Holmes was at home. Told he was not, he went away without leaving a message. So, since he had seen Fiske and knew he had left no note himself they could be reasonably sure no contact had been made."

"So when you got to Fiske's room, the cupboard was bare?"

"Not entirely. The room had been disarranged, though not badly. The writing table had been the main object of his attention, the top sheet of his pad had been roughly torn off and the waste paper basket emptied and discarded. I imagine Fiske had made several efforts to consign his thoughts to paper. It was the disarray that began to arouse the landlady's suspicions. She gave clear signs of wanting to ask some embarrassing questions, until I gave her the benefit of the ale with which I had daubed my person to prevent my having to drink too much of the filthy stuff. There is one virtue of cheap ale, Watson, in the creation of an effective disguise. It tends to linger and create, as it were, a false scent."

"So you came away empty-handed?"

"Oh, I wouldn't go quite that far, my dear fellow." And Holmes retrieved a scrap of paper from the recesses of his voluminous jacket, which he proceeded to smooth flat. From what I could see, it appeared to be totally blank. Holmes caught my questioning expression. "One thing the amateur criminal invariably fails to remember is that to *remove* the message is not to *lose* the message. A writer—particularly someone writing excitedly and in a hurry—will often press down hard on the paper. Thus, the second sheet, always providing one has the appropriate materials to translate it, speaks to us as clearly as the first."

So saying, he rose to his feet, put down the clay pipe without lighting it—for which relief I gave much thanks—and moved over to the table which held his beloved chemical apparatus. There he busied himself for a few minutes, mixing things in a retort and then heating the results in a dish.

Finally, he took a delicate brush and coated the paper. "Come and look at this, Watson . . . now then, Mr Fiske, what have you to say to us from beyond the grave, I wonder?"

Standing at Holmes's shoulder but at a respectful distance from the all-pervasive ale, I watched fascinated as slowly the dead actor's ghostly handwriting appeared . . .

"Dear Mr Holmes—
I must see you. There is much to tell—of words poetic, of Roses and Globes, of shoes and ships and sealing-wax and cabbages and kings. Not to mention Danger. If anyone has doubt of the acoustics of our new home, he need have them no longer. Clarity is all! Considering the stakes, I imagine the labourer will be worthy of his hire? If so, your humble servant stands ready to piece out the imperfection of your thoughts."

And then the flourish of the signature—

E. HAMILTON FISKE

"I think one might safely categorise his style as bravura, on stage or off," Holmes said thought-fully. "He presumably intended to leave this, should he once again find me out in the morning."

"What does he mean about all this 'sealing-wax' nonsense?" I asked.

"Fiske was one of those people who are always 'on'—as actors like to say," Holmes replied. "Nothing was ever simple. He's referring to some nonsense lines from *Alice in Wonderland*, so as to create a playful tone. I don't believe for one moment he thought he was in any danger. On the contrary, he believed he had stumbled on a game in which he held all the worthwhile cards. A little game called blackmail in which he'd sell to the highest bidder. All this tavern talk about his ship coming in. Having missed us, his first and obvious port of call, he may well have decided as the evening wore on that the price of silence would be higher. He just wasn't aware of the real game that was being played out in which he was a mere pawn."

"What do you think happened, Holmes?"

"I fancy we shall find that our 'bearded' young man, satisfied that Fiske had not made the contact he feared, constructed a rapid scenario, brilliant in its simplicity, I must admit. It was generally known that Fiske was an advanced diabetic, I have now ascertained. Prime him with his favourite whisky, which is rich in sugar but can do him little real harm as long as there is the antidote of insulin. But replace the antidote with what he *thinks* is insulin but is, in reality, nothing more than a placebo, and the story is very different."

"And if *that* didn't work?"

"Then a knock on the head in a darkened alley that could hopefully be attributed to a drunken fall. More risky, certainly, but they had no time to devise something of greater finesse. You remember Constable Baker spoke of sensing someone's presence in the square? That, I fancy, was our friend waiting to administer the *coup de grâce* should it prove necessary. As it happened, Plan A sufficed. I would give good odds that we shall find Fiske was dead either just before or just after he mounted his last horse. In either event, his death was 'staged' just as it might have been in a play. And, you know, Watson, the aspect that is beginning to worry me is precisely that theatricality. I'm sure it has not escaped your notice that even the threats are appropriate to the character concerned? 'Cleopatra' is confronted by an asp and 'Richard' loses his earthly kingdom on a horse. There is a perverted touch of—I would almost say genius—at work here that, in other circumstances, would be almost admirable."

A silence fell between us as we pursued our separate thoughts. We'd reached this point often enough in the past and sometimes with even greater violence but it was always a sobering moment to realise that a human life was forfeit and that there was no retreat until the miscreant was brought to book. Even though I knew the adrenalin was coursing through my friend's veins, the look he gave me told me he shared my qualms. This was no longer an amusing crossword puzzle to be laid aside, should it cease to entertain.

It was Holmes who broke the silence. "Time for Act Two, I think, Watson. If you will give me a moment or two to remove the motley, we will again present ourselves as the omniscient investigator and his fearless assistant."

CHAPTER SIX

A n angry voiced echoed through the darkness: "The answer's no, no and if that isn't clear enough for your friends—NO! And you can tell them I'm goddamn tired of talking about it. In case they haven't noticed, I've got a theatre to open and it's going to be *my* theatre!"

It was undoubtedly Florenz Adler's voice we heard as we picked our way through the labyrinth behind the stage towards what was clearly his temporary office. "Do you think we should come back later, Holmes?" I whispered.

"*Carpe diem*, Watson," he smiled and I could see he was enjoying the moment. "When the emotional temperature rises things normally safely hidden have been known to stir." He knocked on the door and with the briefest of pauses we were in the room.

Standing behind the desk and resting his weight on his clenched fists was Adler. A vein throbbed visibly in his temple. Sitting in the chair next to the desk was a youngish bearded man, smoking a cigarette as if he hadn't a care in the world. In fact, he seemed to be positively enjoying himself. He looked up as we came into the room and without bothering to get up, offered a languid hand.

"Good afternoon, Mr Holmes . . . Dr Watson . . .

My father is expecting you. I was merely filling in time until you arrived."

Turning to Adler, he dropped the cigarette on the floor and ground it out under his heel in a way that suggested his calmness was to at least some degree an effort of will. "Well, father, I'm sure you have more than enough to be getting on with. Don't forget the offer stays on the table until the day of the opening. After that, all bets are off. My principals . . ."

"You know exactly what you can tell your principals . . ." shouted Adler, bringing a fist down on the desk. Looking at him now one could see the power he must have commanded on the stage.

The young man nodded, bowed slightly to Holmes and myself and was out of the door. Though I was bursting to speak, I followed my friend's example and stayed silent. Holmes has impressed on me over the years the importance of letting the other person offer the information in the heat of the moment. "Few people can stand the burden of silence and, in order to shed it, they frequently make an ill-considered sacrifice." So it appeared to be with the impresario. He slumped down into his chair and looked at us with a defeated expression. Or was there the merest glint in his eyes of self-possession returning?

"I guess I owe you gentlemen an explanation?" Holmes's expression remained carved in stone.

There was to be no lifeline for Adler from that quarter.

"The young man you just met—not under the most advantageous circumstances, I admit—is my son Henry. By my first marriage," he added. As he spoke, I suddenly recalled the entry in Holmes's index. That would certainly bear further examination, as would the telegrams he had received earlier. I remembered now a reference to a "wife in New York".

"I'm not particularly proud of my earlier life, Mr Holmes," Adler continued. "Like a lot of young men, I was green in judgement and as a strolling player, I suppose I fancied myself quite a fellow. Travel around the country, strut a lot, fret not too much and worry about tomorrow not at all. Way back, when we were both far too young, I'd married a sweet little girl, Iris Tallis, in New York. Then, round about the time I was playing that accursed date in Chicago . . ."

"The one where the President was shot?" I asked.

"That's right, Doctor. *Our American Cousin.* So many things seemed to go off beam after that. Well, as I was saying, it was then that Iris gave birth to our son. I wasn't there, of course. And I guess that tipped the whole balance for her. All the travelling had been getting to her and . . ."—here he dropped his gaze—"all the rumours, I suppose. Anyway, by the time I finally got back to New

York, she'd left and taken the baby with her. She went to a lot of different places, I heard later. I know Canada was one and then she finished up somewhere in England. A year or two later I got a notice to say she'd divorced me. I never saw her again and I'd never laid eyes on Henry until the other day—and I'll come to that in a moment when I've got this off my chest. It's been there a long time, Mr Holmes . . ."

"Pray continue, Mr Adler," Holmes encouraged him and perched himself on the corner of the desk, motioning me to the vacant chair. He clearly had no wish to interrupt Adler's flow.

"I've often wondered what became of them but somehow my own personal demons—guilt, I guess is a better word for it—would never let me make a serious effort to find out. Then, some years ago, I heard that Iris had died in England. At that point I did make some enquiries but by that time the boy was grown and gone. And that was that, gentlemen, until we arrived in England a few weeks ago. One morning I had a visit at my hotel from the representative of some big firm of hot shot lawyers—the name doesn't matter. When he presented his card the name—Henry Tallis— didn't ring a bell right away. Then he told me who he was and you can imagine how I felt. In a funny way *he* seemed to be enjoying it.

" 'Do not upset yourself, Mr Adler,' he said, as cool as may be, 'you won't mind if I don't call you "Father", I'm sure, under the circumstances? I am here strictly in a business capacity.' Then he told me his firm had been retained by a group of theatrical figures in England who had decided—rather late in the day, I might add—that they would now consent to buy me out, so that—as he put it—the Bard might be returned to his rightful owners.

"I'm not good at holding my horses, Mr Holmes—never have been. And being already upset probably made it worse. I lost my temper and told 'Mr Tallis' what he and his principals could do with their offer. They'd had three hundred years to do what I'd done in a couple. I'd even offered to bring them in with me—but no. They wanted nothing to do with this upstart Yankee tourist, until they saw it was actually going to happen. Now I wouldn't touch them with a ten foot pole . . ."

"And when did you see your son again?" Holmes asked quietly.

"I've had a series of reminder notes. Curt little things."

"Written or typed?"

"Typed, I think. I really don't recall. I threw them away. He's also been hanging around the theatre. I've seen him talking to several of the actors. Trying to set them against me, I guess. God, what a mess!" He laughed bitterly. "Not exactly the family reunion you see in plays, I'm afraid."

"How did Mrs Adler take the news?" I asked.

Adler's expression looked for a moment as though he wouldn't answer the question. Then he looked me in the eye. "I'm afraid I haven't plucked up the courage to tell her yet," he replied. "Things have been a little—difficult lately. And, of course, you've heard the dreadful news about Ham Fiske?"

It was as if the specific tragedy of Fiske's death gave him something to hold on to. He stood up and his body seemed to fill out, his batteries to recharge in front of our eyes. "I can't get a straight answer out of the police. What have you heard, Mr Holmes?"

Holmes looked his inscrutable best and I now recalled that in his parting words to Lestrade he had asked that there should be no public announcement for the next few hours, a request to which the bewildered inspector had been only too glad to agree. "I'm afraid we shall all have to wait until the medical report is complete which, I imagine, should be within a matter of hours. Meanwhile, as I believe you theatrical people say, the show must go on, surely?"

It was as if Holmes had given the man a call to arms.

"You're quite right, Mr Holmes. Although that's an old circus phrase—but let's not split hairs. That's precisely what Ham would have wanted. This afternoon we're rehearsing a scene from

Julius Caesar. When we lost Ham, we lost our Caesar as well as our Richard."

The way he said it made it sound like a triple murder and there was little doubt that the fictional characters loomed larger in his mind than the real and recently departed one. It was as if the actor had somehow cheated them and him.

"Luckily, Mr Allan has stepped into his shoes. I'd better be getting over there to see how they're getting on. You gentlemen come on over in your own good time. I fancy you know your way around here by now?" With that he hurried out of the room.

I looked at Holmes. "If I were to say 'The plot thickens', would I be quoting Shakespeare or Wilde? Most things seem to be one or the other."

"I'm afraid you'd lose your money on both scores, old fellow," Holmes replied with a laugh. "I think you'll find it was George Villiers, second Duke of Buckingham. If you're looking for quotations, the one crossing my mind was more on the lines of your fellow Scotsman, Robbie Burns and his 'Oh, what a tangled web we weave . . .' More than one person here is practising to deceive us, old friend."

"Could young Tallis have been the bearded fellow plying Fiske with drink? Perhaps the landlady would recognise him? Adler did say he'd been making up to the actors."

"Possibly," Holmes replied, "but perhaps not

likely. Quite apart from his clients' ambitions, Tallis certainly has his own personal agenda and his own reasons for wanting to see Adler lose face. He's clearly an intelligent young man and though we don't know what he's been doing these past years, apart from qualifying as some sort of solicitor's clerk, I would venture a guess that he's followed his father's recent career with some interest, if not perhaps with the best of intent. The threats? We must certainly add him to our list of suspects where they're concerned. But killing *Fiske?* Too many threads, Watson, too many threads. But we must not waste our time here. I asked Lestrade to meet us and, since punctuality is one of the qualities with which he is cursed, he is almost certainly here by now. The last thing I want is to have him interviewing the actors and telling them more than they tell him!"

Taking my arm, he hustled me through the unfinished corridors and into the yard of the theatre where, sure enough, Lestrade was in conversation with a group of the actors who were not involved in the scene being rehearsed on the stage. "If I didn't know better," Holmes murmured as we approached them, "I'd swear that Lestrade was holding court."

And indeed the inspector did seem in an unusually expansive mood, basking in the attention of Dame Ivy, Pauline French and Carlotta Adler, all of whom appeared to be genuinely fascinated by what he had to say. Seeing us, Lestrade theatrically beckoned us to join the group. "I was just telling these lovely ladies a few of my *own* theatrical experiences, Mr Holmes. There was that very nasty murder at the Brixton Empire a few years ago. You may remember it . . . ?"

"Remember it?" I snorted. "If Holmes hadn't proved that her husband had been introducing arsenic into the leading lady's make-up for months, you'd have arrested her dresser and been the laughing stock of London."

"And then," Lestrade continued, ignoring my interruption as best he could, "another case brought me into contact with Elsie Congreve. Now, there was a lady. The finest actress to grace the English stage . . ."

I looked at Holmes whose expression warned me to keep my peace. And in any case, I would only have been upstaged by Dame Ivy. In his ignorance Lestrade had mentioned the one name that was anathema to her. Every theatregoer knew that the two women were deadly rivals and hadn't spoken for years. Drawing herself up to what appeared to be rather more than her full height, the Dame declared: "She may have *graced* the stage. She certainly never *acted* on it!" It is no mean feat to make an exit from a littered forecourt in full daylight but Dame Ivy managed it to perfection.

It was Holmes who broke the silence that ensued. "Lestrade, a word with you, if I may?"

Over his shoulder I could see Carlotta and Pauline French, suddenly newfound friends, their heads together and giggling like a couple of schoolgirls.

"Ah, yes, Mr Holmes," said Lestrade, patently grateful for the interruption. "I was just trying to distract the ladies from questioning me, like, until you got here."

"So I see."

"Yes, well, the police surgeon gave the body top priority and I've got his report right here." He handed my friend a sheet of paper. "You were quite right. His blood sugar was way past the danger limit. The cause of death was actually cardiac arrest but you'll see that they conclude it was the sudden excess of alcohol that brought it on. We've also checked with his doctor and apparently he's had a number of warnings about this very thing. He's already had several heart attacks and his doctor told him the next one would kill him for sure. Seems he was right. The surgeon also notes that his liver and kidneys were in a right old state. Could have popped off any time."

"Yes, but someone made good and sure he popped off *this* time—*before* his ship came in," Holmes mused. "Thank you, Lestrade. Most helpful."

"And now," Lestrade was peering at the stage, "which of these young chappies is which?" It was, indeed, difficult to tell, since all of them were wearing white Roman togas, except Adler who—

101

perhaps to insist on his own "costume"—still wore his cashmere coat slung around his shoulders.

I pointed out Ted Allan, made up to look older for the part of Caesar . . . Harrison Trent, an open-faced Brutus . . . the slighter figure of Simon Phipps as Cassius. *Did* he have a leaner, hungrier look since yesterday or was I reading into his face what I thought I knew of last night's events? As for the rest of the group they were unknown to me—spear or, in this case, dagger carriers.

Finally, Adler seemed satisfied that they had understood his direction and stepped back, signalling the actors to continue. "Let's take it from—'I could be well moved' . . ."

Allan made his entrance from behind one of the stage pillars and once again I found myself marvelling at the actor's art. He carried his slender frame as though it had suddenly added several pounds and as many years. His walk was now heavy. For that moment he *was* a Roman emperor.

> I could be well mov'd if I were as you;
> If I could pray to move, prayers would
>   move me:
> But I am constant as the northern star,
> Of whose true-fix'd and resting quality
> There is no fellow in the firmament . . .

There was no doubt about it, the man was impressive. I turned to Holmes, only to find an expression I recognised all too well. His face had that pinched look that came over it when he sensed something was wrong. "What is it, Holmes?" I whispered.

"Probably nothing," he said, speaking so that only I could hear, "but doesn't it occur to you that, if last night's attempt had failed—which let us not forget, was a last minute improvisation—this was an ideal and prearranged moment when Fiske was *supposed* to be killed on stage—another Shakespearean murder."

"But no one *needs* to kill Fiske now. Fiske is dead."

"Just so, but the original scenario still holds. Adler is still determined to go ahead and open the theatre . . ."

> But there's but one in all doth hold his place:
> So, in the world; 'tis furnished well with
>   men,
> And men are flesh and blood and
>   apprehensive;
> Yet in the number I do know but one
> That unassailable holds on his rank
> Unshak'd of motion . . .

"So . . . ?"

"So perhaps our friend—now our killer—will choose to use the Ides of March after all to press his point."

On the stage an outraged Caesar—for I no longer thought of him as Ted Allan—spoke his penultimate line . . .

Doth not Brutus bootless kneel?

On cue the actor playing Casca cried: "Speak, hands, for me!" and the crowd of actors surrounded the figure of Caesar like a flock of white carrion crows. At which point Holmes gripped my arm with painful strength. For instead of the line which every schoolboy knows—"Et tu, Brute? Then fall, Caesar!" an unearthly voice from that crowd was heard to shout—"Wither one rose and let the other flourish!"

"Come, Watson," I heard Holmes cry, "there's not a moment to lose!"

Luckily, there was a builder's scaffold in place by the stage and we were up and running across it in a moment. I shall never forget the sight of that frozen tableau and the deathly silence that fell over the theatre. Adler looked like Lot's wife, rooted to the spot, his mouth agape. Even the workmen had ceased whatever they were doing.

Slowly the white clad figures moved back—all except one. Lying on the ground was the figure of Ted Allan with blood beginning to spread over his white toga. I'm not an imaginative man by nature, as Holmes will attest, but it reminded me of nothing so much as a red rose opening its petals.

I was conscious of Holmes at my side, saying

urgently, "Your department, I think, Watson." I knelt and picked up Allan's outstretched hand, feeling for the pulse. It seemed strong enough and then he began to stir. Taking out the penknife that had served me well in many a far flung spot over the years, I quickly slit the cotton of his toga and examined the wound.

"This gentleman appears to have been luckier than the character he was playing." I looked up at Holmes, who was examining something in his hand which he held in his handkerchief. "The blood makes it look worse than it is. He seems to have been nicked in the side and the shock has done the rest." Then what I had said struck me. "But surely they were using prop daggers?"

"All, it seems, except one," Holmes replied, holding up the object he had been studying—a small but lethal looking antique dagger with unmistakable evidence of fresh blood on the blade. "No trace of fingerprints," he continued, answering my unspoken question. "Whoever used it was careful to wrap it in the folds of his toga."

I was aware of Carlotta Adler at my elbow holding out some sort of first aid kit. "Here, Dr Watson, this may at least help you to clean the wound until the ambulance gets here. I've sent off the boy in a cab. Luckily, there's a hospital quite close by."

A few minutes later I had Allan safely bandaged up. In fact, he had suffered little more than a fairly deep scratch. He was now fully conscious and apologetic, as so many of the injured are, for causing us all trouble. "Stupid accident," wincing slightly as the hospital orderlies carefully moved him on to a stretcher, "somebody must have mixed up the props back stage. Have to be more careful on the night."

"That's right," said Holmes, "the obvious explanation. Take good care of our star, gentlemen, he has many more parts to play." As the orderlies negotiated their way off the stage, my friend then did a curious thing. He moved quickly to the spot where Allan had been lying, then bent down to tie a shoe lace that didn't appear to need tying. Only I noticed him scoop up a piece of paper which must have been under Allan's body.

After the real life drama a form of normality began to reassert itself. The Roman actors stood upstage in an anxious group, conversing in low tones. Elsewhere builders and stage hands were gradually picking up their various tasks where they had left them. Holmes and I walked over to where Adler was standing with a protective arm round his wife. It was as if the shock of events had broken down some sort of barrier between them and they were seeking each other out for mutual comfort. Carlotta looked strained but perfectly composed and, in fact, it was she who spoke first.

"I've been urging Flo to give up this whole

venture, Mr Holmes. Or at least cancel the opening. Can't *you* reason with him? I just know more terrible things are going to happen."

I looked at Adler and saw the conflicting emotions playing in his eyes. For the first time I saw him undecided, as he turned and looked Holmes full in the eye. "Mr Holmes," he said in a quiet voice, devoid of any theatrical mannerism, "nobody has ever called me a quitter but I confess to you, I just don't know what to do for the best. My gut instinct tells me to go ahead and let the devil take the hindmost. But then, Lotta's quite right—I *am* responsible for all these people." He swept his arm around the "wooden O" to encompass the theatre and everyone in it. "And being a foreigner and all, do I have the *right* to take any further chances? Whoever is behind all this certainly means business. There's no doubt about that now."

Holmes handed him the scrap of paper he had picked up from the stage. "Before you make your mind up, Mr Adler, perhaps you should read your correspondent's latest missive. This one is addressed to you personally." And indeed, as Holmes passed it to the impresario, I could see the name typed on the outer fold. Almost tentatively, Adler unfolded the paper and perused its contents. His jaw muscles tightened and he was about to tear the paper into fragments when Carlotta Adler snatched it from him and read it aloud . . .

THIS VISITATION IS BUT TO WHET THY ALMOST BLUNTED PURPOSE
Hamlet

"The ghost of Hamlet's father," Holmes murmured, almost to himself. "He's trying to tell us that, like a ghost, he can appear among us whenever he feels like it. And indeed, he does appear to possess a certain wraithlike quality." Then, turning to Adler: "You asked me for my opinion. While the shape of events is becoming steadily clearer to me, I am not yet ready to attempt an explanation. In the past I have been tempted—occasionally even flattered by events—into seeking a complex explanation when a simpler one was close by and infinitely more likely. Few things turn out to be as unnatural as the commonplace and nothing more deceptive than the obvious fact. I sense that to be true in this case."

"You above all, Mr Adler, must be aware of the seductive power of theatrical artifice. You spend your life willing people to think they see something when in reality it is something else. Our killer—or killers—is engaged in just such a piece of theatre and we are his intended audience. But strip away the smoke and mirrors of illusion and what are the facts? His timetable is precisely the same as yours but you have momentum on your side. Unless he can arrest that momentum, the theatre will open and he, as he sees it, will have lost. Furthermore, as the sand runs faster through the hourglass, he will become more desperate."

"But, Mr Holmes, that's just what I've been telling Flo," Carlotta interposed, tightening her hold on Adler's arm. "That's why we have to call it off before he tries to kill him, too."

"In my judgement, Mrs Adler, your husband is the *one* person whose life is not in the slightest danger," Holmes replied. "The main objective is to leave the Globe dark and empty and Florenz Adler personally and professionally humiliated. To achieve that end he must be alive for the killer to derive that satisfaction. Everything else is incidental. However, if I may continue with my train of thought . . ."

Carlotta had been on the point of saying something more but thought better of it.

"It is too easy to talk as though our adversary is moving us around like pawns in a game of chess of his own devising and in which he makes all the moves. Yet the facts suggest otherwise. Fiske's death, though made to *look* dramatic, was a dangerously *ad hoc* business and I detect a certain panic creeping into the playing. His choice of quotations, for instance, is beginning to be less considered or indeed, apt . . ." He indicated the paper Carlotta still held crumpled in her hand.

"The 'almost blunted purpose' Hamlet's father

is referring to is Hamlet's intention to kill Claudius, his uncle and his father's murderer. Your 'purpose' is supposedly to cease and desist from opening this theatre. The connection, though clear enough, is quite a tenuous one.

"You ask me for my advice," Holmes said, fixing the couple with a direct gaze that brooked no argument. "It is this. There is more at stake here than your personal pride—or, indeed, mine. Nothing would induce me to suggest you give best to someone who hides behind such threadbare theatrics. He has written the first two acts but we shall write the play's finale. To do that we must encourage him to think that his tactics are working. Today is Friday. The theatre is to open next Tuesday, so we have four days. I suggest when Watson and I have left you call the cast together and tell them you are considering cancelling the opening . . ."

"But, Mr Holmes . . . !" Adler's expression was a mixture of anger and incomprehension. "I thought you said . . . ?"

"Bear with me. You will *say* that you are considering the option. They are not to worry for, whatever you decide, their salaries will be paid in full. You will invite them to join you for dinner at your hotel on Sunday evening, when you will expect to hear their various points of view and come to your decision. Mrs Adler here will let it be known later that one possibility you are considering is to sell out to the group whose interests your son represents. None of this, needless to say," Holmes raised a hand to forestall further interruption, "will be your true intent. However, it will both buy us time and lull our man into a sense of false security. I suggest you do this without delay, now that what remains of your cast seems to be complete."

He indicated the group of actors, who had now been joined by Dame Ivy and Pauline French and were whispering and looking nervously in our direction.

"I'll do as you say, Mr Holmes," said Adler and you could see him bracing himself to resume his usual role, "but, of course, our party won't be complete. Poor Ted . . ."

"Oh, I think you'll find that Mr Allan will not only be in the land of the living but back amongst you after a good night's rest in St Bart's. You should certainly lay a place for him on Sunday. Watson and I will also joint you, if you will have us and one more thing . . ."

"What is that?"

"I should also invite Henry Tallis. Nothing could give greater credence to your story than to see the Trojan Horse within the gates by invitation."

Adler looked as though he was about to expostulate but the pressure of Carlotta's hand on his arm caused him to think better of it. With an abrupt nod he began to cross the stage towards the actors. With every step he seemed to fill out, until by the time he reached them he was the old Flo Adler again, throwing arms round shoulders, his voice booming with energy.

I turned back to address Mrs Adler. Her attention was totally fixed on her husband, her expression a mixture of anxiety and admiration. It was Holmes who broke the silence. "You are married to a remarkable man, Mrs Adler. He deserves to have his dream come true and, God willing, we shall make sure that it does. Now, if you'll forgive us . . ."

"Of course, Mr Holmes. And I must go and see what news there is from the hospital." Then, as he was turning to go, she plucked at his sleeve. "Mr Holmes . . . ?" She was almost beseeching in her tone. "There is something I must discuss with you but not here. May I call on you both later?"

"We shall be delighted, dear lady, shall we not, Watson? Let us say six o'clock?" Tipping his hat, he led the way to the back of the stage. As I followed close behind, I took a last look. Carlotta stood like a tragic Wagnerian heroine leaning against one of the massive pillars, while on the far side of the stage were the rest of the cast, huddled together like the conspirators many of them had so recently played. In the centre of the stage, now dried to a muddy brown, was the pool of blood that indicated a drama more real than Shakespeare had ever intended for it.

"A penny for your thoughts, Watson?" It was Holmes waiting for me in the shadow cast by the late afternoon sunlight.

"Two things, really," I answered, as we walked towards the entrance. "Somehow the people and the characters they're supposed to be playing are running together in my mind, so it's getting hard to tell who's acting and who's not. And then Allan's stab wound. There was something very strange about that and I don't mean that it was caused by a real dagger . . ."

"You mean that when one man strikes at another with a knife—as the conspirators did at Caesar— he strikes the blow downwards. Whereas the blow that Allan suffered was struck upwards? And to make things even more awkward, I believe that, should there have been a corpse for a pathologist to examine, he would have deduced that it was delivered by a left handed man using his right hand to further obscure the facts. Our friend Allan, I am prepared to wager, stabbed himself."

"Yes," I said almost stopping in my tracks. "Exactly. But that's impossible!"

"No, old friend—merely improbable. When one cannot conceive the end result, it becomes difficult to see the connections. Here, we have no such problem. For reasons we have yet to fathom, friend Allan simply wishes to remove himself from our list of suspects."

By this time we were emerging into the street,

when a woman's voice called out to us. Turning my head, I saw Dame Ivy hurrying towards us. "Mr Holmes, I must speak with you."

Her tone was a far remove from the poised and icy lady we had seen hitherto and by her bearing the years seemed suddenly to have caught up with her. "It must stop, I tell you—it must *stop!*"

"What must stop?" said Holmes, holding out a hand to steady her. But the Dame said no more. Instead, her eyes fixed on something beyond us and in them was an expression of stark terror.

Turning to find the object of her attention, I saw an ambulance drawn up to the nearby kerb. Two uniformed attendants were in the act of loading a stretcher into the open back of it. On the stretcher, propped up on one arm, was the incongruous figure of Ted Allan, the bloodstained toga looking like nothing so much as a winding sheet.

But it was the expression on his face that rivetted my attention. The eyes turned in our direction were fixed and cold, like those of a corpse. And then I realised that Allan was only looking at one of us. "*What* must stop, Dame Ivy?" I heard Holmes repeat but there was no answer. When I turned, it was to see her scurrying back down the passage towards the stage.

CHAPTER SEVEN

Holmes and I were sitting on either side of the fireplace in Baker Street. Mrs Hudson had cleared away the tea things and, since there was an unseasonable chill in the air, had lit the fire. Holmes was sitting wreathed in clouds of tobacco smoke, a languid look on his face that told me he was pleased with the way the case was progressing. For the life of me I failed to see why but then I had long since ceased to be concerned by my own inadequacies in dealing with that remarkable mind.

"Come, Holmes," I said, "we have both witnessed the same events and heard the same conversations, yet I am as much in the dark as when the whole business started. How could you be so confident with the Adlers?"

"I grant that I perhaps overdid things but in my experience actors—particularly those of the—shall we say?—more emphatic persuasion, such as Florenz Adler undoubtedly is, are happiest with broad brush strokes. Within the confines of these four walls I can confess to you, Watson, that there are many aspects of the case that still elude me, despite the fact that I do have more information at my disposal than you." He brandished a sheaf of telegrams. "These arrived while you were attending to your toilet after our return."

I held up my hand when he offered them to me. "Just give me the gist."

"Much as I trust those splendid folk at Scotland Yard, I thought it advisable to pursue my own separate enquires through my old friend, John Summers of Pinkertons. I was able to be of some small assistance to him in the Wells Fargo forgery case. Perhaps you remember it but no, I believe it was while you were off on one of your marital sabbaticals.

"In any event," he skimmed through the papers, "he has been able to turn up some of the more recent information about certain of our cast of characters and their exploits in the United States.

"Dame Ivy we already know about, though Summers further postulates that she may well have lent Adler money during his earlier, impoverished years. Even though one imagines the money has long since been paid back and Adler has employed her consistently . . ."

"The real debt can never be repaid? Woman scorned and all that, eh?" I added.

"Precisely. And obviously now susceptible to someone whose motives are strong and more immediate than her own and who has undoubtedly offered to either put money in her purse or expose her past, leaving the lady little choice . . .

"No, Watson, our Grande Dame is strictly a supporting player. We must look elsewhere for the leader."

"What about this fellow Phipps? He's mixed up in it, surely?"

"Ah yes, Phipps. Summers has something to say about him. As I prophesied, he is far from being what he purports to be. His early history is unclear but the first trace Pinkertons have of him is when he joined a touring acting troupe some two years ago, helping out in general and playing small parts. It seems the talent Adler spoke of became evident and he was soon playing leading roles. The general feeling was that he was a fine young actor but emotionally unstable, particularly when in drink. A year or so ago there was an incident in a bar in San Francisco involving a lady's honour and a man was killed. Witnesses contradicted one another and there was insufficient evidence to hold Phipps—though he wasn't using that name at the time. He seems to have left the country right away and soon after that, arrived back in England, where he took on the persona we see today."

"Is he our man?" I asked. "We know he was one of the two men with Fiske that night . . ."

"Yes, but we also know that he was seconded late in the game and seemed ill-prepared for his part. Furthermore, his history suggests that he is someone quick to anger, rather than a careful planner and, whatever else we may deduce about our literary friend, we must grant him a degree of organisational skill. No, Watson, I fancy we shall find that Master Simon will fall into the same category as Dame Ivy. Both are victims of someone who knows something about them they have gone to great pains to cover up and live down."

"Which leaves us with . . . ?"

"Which leaves us with Harrison 'Harry' Trent and Summers has some interesting information for us about that young man. We knew his father was an old colleague of Adler's and sometime competitor. What we didn't know was that it was Adler who caused his death . . ."

"But how . . . ?"

"Addison Trent was never more than a poor second to Adler. In the late 1880s he borrowed heavily to stage the production that was to re-establish his reputation. *This England* was apparently a magnificent re-staging of Shakespeare's history plays and it was playing to capacity audiences when the lease of the theatre came up for renewal. In a bitter auction it passed to . . ."

"Florenz Adler?"

"The very same. Adler wanted the theatre to stage a revue starring his wife, Carlotta. As the new owner he evicted Trent, who could find no other theatre suitable for his production. He had to close it and declare himself bankrupt. After that, he was never able to raise money again. Six years ago he blew his brains out and left a note blaming Adler for his troubles. It made headlines in the New York papers but in America, unfortunately, such things seem commonplace. Today few people remember."

"Except Harrison Trent . . . and, of course, Florenz. His hiring his old friend's son is presumably his way of trying to atone. Whether young Trent sees it in the same light is, of course, open to question."

"Which leaves us with Ted Allan . . ."

"And there, I'm afraid, the good Summers has drawn a temporary blank. He hopes to get back to me within the next day or so and he has never failed me yet. Tell me, Watson, does it not strike you as strange that here we have three young men—Phipps, Trent and Allan—all of an age, all of whom seem to emerge from their own personal shadows at around the same time in the same place and all of whom come together in *this* place, at *this* time, as if drawn to a magnet called Florenz Adler?"

"Not to mention Henry Tallis, Adler's son. There's another coincidence for you. I say, Holmes—you don't think they could all be in this together, do you?"

"A conspiracy? All for one and one for all, like Monsieur Dumas's musketeers? A captivating thought, Watson, that would make excellent material for one of your imaginative narratives. I can see it now. We find our suspects in some enclosed environment—a country house, perhaps, or even a luxury train, like the Orient Express.

It transpires that they murder the victim in concert, so that no one of them is guilty. However, somehow I find that explanation a little rich for my blood in the present situation. No, there is *one* mind guiding these events."

"Just a moment, Holmes," I interrupted, "we've forgotten someone . . ."

"Carlotta, you mean?" Holmes replied. "Not forgotten, old friend, merely a lady in waiting. We shall soon be able to hear that lady's story ourselves." So saying, he pulled out his watch and opened the case. "Six o'clock precisely and there is the lady's finger on the bell."

"I'm sure you're right on this occasion," I teased him, "but how can you be so infernally sure it isn't a telegram boy or some friend of Mrs Hudson's?"

"I have learned over the years, Watson, that our front door bell speaks a language all its own. There is the faint, almost fugitive touch of the visitor who is in two minds as to whether he should share his—or frequently her—problems with a stranger. There is the imperious ring of the outraged victim prepared to wait not a moment longer for redress at whatever cost to our bell pull. And there is the resigned ring—of which we have just heard a good example—which tells of someone who knows they have no alternative. Ah, Miss Mencken, do come in, please . . ."

The woman who had been in the act of entering the room froze like a statue, her hand on the door knob. She was dressed from head to foot in black and veiled. I was instantly reminded of the identical figure whose arrival had set the present events in motion—what was it?—but two short days ago. But this woman was altogether smaller in stature and more womanly than our earlier visitor, whom we now knew to have been Dame Ivy and when she lifted the veil from her face, we were looking at the stricken face of Carlotta Adler. Except why had Holmes addressed her as "Miss Mencken"?

"So you know everything, Mr Holmes. How could I expect to hide it from you?" Her voice was harsh and pained, very different from the tones that had pierced the hearts of thousands in concert halls all over the world. Sensing her distress, I guided her to the visitors' chair. She sank into it gratefully and looked at us with tear-filled eyes that still retained some defiance. Carlotta Adler may not have been *the* woman but she was certainly a woman to be reckoned with and Holmes immediately acknowledged as much as he answered her.

"Mrs Adler, please forgive an unworthy remark on my part. I can promise you I am far from omniscient, as my friend Watson here will certainly tell you. In fact, as far as you are concerned, I know no more than these telegrams from America tell me, which is what anyone with access to public records may discover."

I felt that Holmes was being a little economical with the truth here but I bit back the remark that sprang to my lips. When he determined to put a witness at their ease, there was none to match him and the old magic seemed to be working once more.

"I sometimes foresee a day when all of us will be reduced to a set of facts and figures at the mercy of some infernal machine," Holmes continued with a smile that coaxed something like a response in kind from Carlotta Adler. Picking up his mood, I added: "And presumably that day will mark the end of the investigator? Who will need you and I when they have a machine?"

At this Holmes laughed out loud. "Watson, I do declare that subversive sense of humour of yours will be the end of me! I don't think we need to worry that this will come to pass in our lifetime and, in any case—if I may quote myself—I can conceive of a machine that may *see* but never one that *observes*."

"Thank you, Mr Holmes," Carlotta said softly. "You, too, Doctor Watson. The last few days have been a strain, as you know all too well. But it is the things only I know that are threatening my sanity. I must share them with someone . . ."

"Watson and I are at your service, madam."

"It all began in Washington after we moved there from Florida. I was an only child, spoiled beyond belief, I'm sure. And you're quite right,

Mr Holmes, the family name *was* Mencken. Charlotte Mencken—the girl everyone said was pretty, the girl everyone said was a talented singer who would go far. But mere I was—18, 19 and not going anywhere. Until the *actors* came to town . . ."

For a moment she said nothing more, as she seemed to gather her thoughts. Then the colour began to rise in cheeks that had no need of rouge. She continued, not quite meeting Holmes's eye.

"I'm not proud of the way I behaved, Mr Holmes. I thought I was a sophisticated woman of the world, when all the time I was a silly little provincial girl. Flo Adler and his friend, Addy Trent were the sort of people I'd never met in my life before. They'd been everywhere and seen everything, to hear them tell it. They laughed at everything, they lived it up and, once I'd met them, they insisted on taking me along for the ride. The three of us were inseparable and a lot of local eyebrows were raised but I just ignored them. This was the Theatre. This was life. Both with capital letters.

"I adored them both but Flo was the one for me. I'd never met a man like him. I still haven't. Oh, sure, I knew he was married but he said his wife didn't understand him—how many times have I heard that line since?—And, in any case, we 'women of the world' don't live by other people's rules. I guess that shows you how green

123

I was. He told me about his romance with Ivy, too, but even that didn't worry me. We didn't make any commitments. When the circus left town, that would be that. And, of course, after that terrible business . . . there was no more circus."

By now two large tears were running down her cheeks. Once again I found myself offering my bandana to a Miss Adler and this time the offer was accepted.

"Perhaps I can ease the burden a little, Mrs Adler." Holmes leaned forward in his chair and laid a surprisingly gentle hand on her arm. "Soon after Adler left you found you were expecting his child. To prevent the imminent scandal, your parents sent you off to live with an aunt in Seattle until the baby was born and could be given over for adoption. It was a son, I believe?"

"But how could you . . . ?"

"I have my methods, Mrs Adler, and some rather effective sources of information, which, I might add, are totally discreet. You need not distress yourself further with that aspect of your story but I fancy this is not the only thing you came to tell us?"

Carlotta continued as though Holmes had not spoken.

"I never told Flo at the time and I haven't told him to this day. It was weak of me, I know, and I've suffered for it more rather than less as the years have gone by and I've wondered—'Where is my son *now? Who* is my son now?' But then I tell myself all that happened to a different person. You see, when I was—'convalescing' in Seattle, I filled in the time by taking more singing lessons. One thing led to another and before long I was singing professionally. The rest you know. I met up with Flo again in New York years later. By that time he was divorced. He started to manage my career and eventually we decided to get married. It wasn't the mad romance we both remembered but we've been together a while now and the good things outweighed the bad. I wouldn't want to see him hurt.

"Flo's never said anything to me about his son, Henry, even though you've only to see the two of them together to know the truth. I guess he'll tell me in his own good time and if he doesn't, well, what's past is past. I'd be keeping my own secrets, too—or trying to—were it not for this . . ." And she fumbled for a moment in her handbag before producing the familiar folded scrap of white paper. "This one was waiting for me in our hotel the day we arrived. Luckily, Flo was too busy checking the arrangements to ask me about it."

She handed it to Holmes and I moved my chair nearer to his so that I could read it with him. The same typewritten characters, the same bold outline of a rose—a symbol that seemed to become more mesmeric each time I saw it. The text read . . .

—WHOSE SON ART THOU?
—MY MOTHER'S SON, SIR.
—THY MOTHER'S SON! LIKE ENOUGH,
AND THY FATHER'S SHADOW.

Henry IV, Pt.2

"And what did you take it to mean?" Holmes looked at her keenly.

"What else *could* it mean? My son had found out who his mother was and was intent on punishing me in some way for my past actions. Why otherwise would he not make himself known to me directly without this strange charade? I didn't know what to do, Mr Holmes. The one person I would naturally have told was the one person I could *not* tell. I was horribly torn. On the one hand I wanted to *see* my son, if this was indeed a message from him and not some cruel hoax. On the other, I feared his motives and the loss of the life I now had, even though it was in a sense at his expense. I was not proud of the emotions that overwhelmed me. And then the other day—the day you and Doctor Watson first came to the Globe—*this* arrived . . ."

She now produced a second note and passed it across. It read . . .

COME, SIT DOWN EVERY MOTHER'S SON. REHEARSE YOUR PARTS.

A Midsummer Night's Dream

"The tone grows more threatening," Holmes mused, as he compared the two notes, "and the patience wears thinner, as the desired response is not forthcoming. Look at the penmanship on the later rose, Watson. The final swirl is an angry flourish that almost tears the paper. The lines are clumsy, which presumably adds to his frustration."

His analysis was a subtlety that was largely lost on Carlotta Adler, preoccupied as she was with her own problems. "Now you see why I'm so anxious for Flo to pull back even at this late hour and even though I know he thinks I'm being disloyal. Call it my woman's instinct, gentlemen, but I feel this man—whether he is my son or not—means us genuine harm and I fear that recent events have proved me right. You must find him, Mr Holmes, find him before it's too late. If it's money he wants, well, I have a little . . ."

"I very much doubt that we shall find money plays any part in his calculations. And, if it's any slight assurance to you, Mrs Adler, I suspect that should the biological connection that you suspect exist, that is a contributory but not a principal factor in this affair. If a particular man had not decided to build a particular playhouse, skeletons—if you'll pardon the expression—could have stayed firmly locked in their cupboards. Rest assured, my dear lady, that Watson and I will spare no effort to bring this distressing business to a speedy resolution."

"What can I do to help, Mr Holmes?"

"Watch and listen for the smallest details of behaviour that diverge from the normal pattern. Omit nothing. Watson here has lost count of the times that I have counselled him on the subject. The truth is invariably to be found in the details, in the smallest of brush strokes. Other than that, go about your normal business and give that husband of yours the moral support that he needs. You indicate that he has his faults but then, which of us does not? If I were to ask Watson to list mine, the great Globe would be open long before he had finished!"

"Mr Holmes, Doctor Watson, I can't thank you enough."

Carlotta Adler was now dabbing at her face with those instruments that women invariably carry and never forget to use, no matter how severe the crisis. "And here am I inundating you with *my* troubles without even telling you the good news. Ted Allan is going to be fine. As you diagnosed, Doctor, it was little more than a nick. Being in a fleshy part of the hip, it bled a lot and that made it look worse. He's a lucky young man. He might have been . . ."

She stopped abruptly in the realisation of what she'd been about to say. The effect was theatrical, even operatic. The diva open mouthed with powder puff poised, an aria imminent. Instead, she said very quietly—"*One* of those young men is a murderer. He is also my son. And that is a terrible thought to live with. Goodnight, gentlemen."

A few moments later we heard the street door close behind her. For a minute or two Holmes and I sat there looking into the fire, each of us nursing our own thoughts. Finally, I said—"Well, in the light of that little revelation, Phipps is our man after all, surely? Right age. Appears from nowhere. American background as well as English. Used to playing parts. In the blood, I shouldn't wonder."

"True. But then, so is Allan. And there we have the advantage of the lady. She rules him out of her calculations because she classifies him as a victim but, if that should happen to be a role—however painful . . .

"And there is one other small fact which I omitted to mention, old fellow. Harrison Trent was adopted. I've asked Pinkertons to check into the adoption agency."

"You mean Trent was so in love with Carlotta that he found out about the child and took it for his own?"

"Watson, how often do I have to remind you that to infer from insufficient data is the capital crime of the investigative mind? All we know is that at this moment there are three viable candidates.

"And there is one other thing that, fortunately, has so far not occurred to Carlotta Adler—another irony of Shakespearean proportions."

"And that is?"

"You remember the last quotation Adler received? The line about the 'almost blunted purpose'? In this case Claudius and Hamlet's father are one and the same man. A fact that only we and Mrs Adler know. And now, if you would be kind enough to pick up the book from the third shelf above your elbow, I should like to consult the deathless prose of that publication that contains inspiration second only to the Good Book itself."

"If you mean *Bradshaw*, why don't you say so?" I replied crossly, tossing him the red covered tome that had occupied so many of his waking hours since I had known him. "What is this evening's text?"

"The morning trains to Oxford."

"And who is going to Oxford, pray?"

"*We* are—at the crack of tomorrow's dawn. It is time we learned all there is to know about roses . . ."

CHAPTER EIGHT

By the time the dreaming spires had tolled the hour of ten, I found myself in the middle of an Oxford tutorial.

"Mr Holmes, my work constantly requires me to study the image, then seek the meaning behind it. In that I suspect we are not dissimilar. I know much of you—admittedly, at second hand. What does your limited acquaintance tell you about me?"

"Relatively little, I'm afraid. Other than the fact that you have two Siamese cats, are a keen but not particularly successful fly fisherman, prefer the works of Trollope to those of Dickens and have recently taken a long walk along the Isis towpath, I know only what I have been told by others— that you are the leading expert in the field of Elizabethan and Jacobean theatre practice."

There was a silence as the interrogator looked at Holmes over his half glasses. Professor Campbell Bryson of Balliol College, Oxford was a thin man of medium height whose habit of sitting hunched up in his winged leather chair made him look smaller. Despite that, he dominated his environment, as I have no doubt he fully intended to do. I could well imagine generations of undergraduates sitting opposite his book and paper-encrusted desk transfixed by that beady eye. The rest of his study was littered with similar piles, to the point where one had to negotiate the stacks with care to avoid the possibility of starting an avalanche. Dust covered most of the surfaces yet one had the sense that Bryson could lay his hand on anything he wanted without a moment's hesitation. The room was designed to create a particular effect as, indeed, was the professor's tactic of opening the conversation to take the other person off guard. It was a typical don's gambit but he had picked the wrong opponent in Holmes.

At last he was forced to indulge his curiosity. When he did so, a boyish smile lit up his face. The academic disappeared and the real man appeared as he unclasped his hands from behind his head and sat forward in his chair. "I see your reputation combines image *and* content. Now please put me out of my misery."

"My profession is based on the observation of detail, Professor, and the details in your case are obvious enough. You wear a coarse tweed jacket which, by the way the cuffs and elbows are patched, is obviously a favourite that you wear constantly. There are two distinct types of cat's hairs adhering to it—a silvery grey and a marmalade gold—that suggest the presence of pedigree and almost certainly Siamese cats rubbing themselves against you—a practice which, if you were not a cat lover, you would never allow . . ."

"*Touché*! My wife is always chastising me for not brushing this jacket but life is too short for such niceties. But what about the fishing? You spotted the hat on the coatrack as you came in, no doubt?"

"Yes, the number and variety of flies in the hatband tell of the keenness to participate in the sport but the mounted fish on the bookcase tells the real story. Don't think me rude, Professor, but to mount a fish which most anglers would have thrown back suggests enthusiasm verging on desperation."

At this, Bryson threw his head back and laughed until the tears came, at the same time banging his hand on the desk enthusiastically, sending up a cloud of dust that hung around his head, catching the sunlight. It was a strange and spectral sight.

"As for the rest of my little parlour trick," Holmes continued, "I am almost ashamed to own up to it. The collected works of Messrs Dickens and Trollope are sitting next to each other on that shelf and whereas the Trollopes show signs of being well used, those of Mr Dickens look almost pristine in their bindings. I agree with your literary verdict, by the way. The walk down the towpath? Something of a guess on my part, I must confess. The burrs that have fastened themselves to your trousers and jacket cuffs are to be found in profusion among the vegetation that lines the river bank at this time of the year and knowing you to be a fisherman . . ."

"*Quod erat demonstrandum*, Mr Holmes," said the professor, wiping his eyes on a none too clean kerchief. "You have made my day, I do declare. Now, what can I do to assist yours and Dr Watson's? Your telegram was elliptical, to say the least."

"Before I get to that, Professor, may I thank you for interrupting your weekend and . . ." nodding towards the trophy case, "particularly your fishing, in order to see Dr Watson and myself. We will try to take up as little of your time as possible, since I have every reason to believe that the information we seek is at your mental fingertips. A matter which my friend and I are currently investigating has certain connections with the newly rebuilt Globe playhouse . . ."

Bryson nodded, his interest now fully engaged. "Yes, I've been following it with great interest, as you may imagine. Adler even consulted me when the project was in its elephantine gestation period—as I believe he consulted everyone with any pretension to academic status. When my opinion differed from his, I'm afraid I was banished like Prospero. A single-minded man, Mr Adler.

"Having said that, I admire much, indeed most, of what he has finally realised on Bankside. The great Globe once more rises to be—in Ben

134

Jonson's deathless description—'the glorie of the Banke'. So, yes—to respond in my tortuous scholar's way—I know about the Globe. In all three of its incarnations . . ."

"Three?" I felt obliged to ask, having made myself a mental promise to be a passive observer to what promised to be an exchange far above my intellectual level. Curiosity, however, got the better of discretion. "There were *three* Globes?"

"Indeed, there were, Doctor," said Bryson, turning his head in my direction for the first time since we had been introduced. "Or should I be pedantically academic and say 'will be', since the third is shortly to be with us? The first Globe was built on a site a few yards from the present structure under somewhat 'romantic' circumstances, if that isn't too imprecise a word. James Burbage, an Elizabethan theatrical impresario, not unlike our mutual acquaintance, Florenz Adler, built a playhouse north of the river in Shoreditch. It was a wooden building circular in shape and he called it simply the Theatre—from the Greek *teatron* or 'viewing place'. In it he staged plays for his troupe of actors, The Lord Chamberlain's Men, a troupe which included his son, Richard and later, a young actor who also wrote plays . . ."

"Will Shakespeare?"

"Will Shakespeare. The very same. Well, James Burbage died, the lease of the Theatre expired and the landlord refused to renew it, so Richard, his brother, Cuthbert, Shakespeare and the rest of the troupe—with the help of a master builder, Peter Streete, simply dismantled the timbers one December night in 1599 and transported them across the river to a site they had already leased in Southwark. It was the origin of the 'moonlight flit'. At least, one *hopes* it was by moonlight . . ." He smiled at the telling of a tale that was clearly more real to him than most of the things that happened in his daily life. "Forgive me, gentlemen, didactic discourse is second nature in the groves of academe . . ."

"Please continue," Holmes encouraged him, "the story is fascinating and you tell it as though it were happening yesterday."

Thus encouraged, the Professor went on. "They called their new playhouse built with the old timbers—The Globe. You remember Shakespeare's line 'All the world's a stage'? . . ."

"Shakespeare's lines are much on our minds lately, are they not, Watson?" Holmes murmured, anxious not to stop Bryson's flow.

"The Burbages, Shakespeare and a handful of others were 'sharers' in the new company. In other words, they had a financial interest in its affairs and decided its policy. Shakespeare himself, of course, became their principal playwright and most of his great plays—*Hamlet*, *Othello*, *Twelfth Night*, *Macbeth*, *King Lear*—were written specifically for 'this wooden "O"', as he called it, most of them with Richard Burbage in the leading role. It must have been a magnificent time . . ."

His eyes were far away, three hundred years away as he spoke. Suddenly, realising he had not even begun to answer my original question, he pulled himself back to the present. When he continued, his tone was crisper.

"The first Globe was burned down in 1613. During a production of *Henry VIII* a prop cannon on stage malfunctioned. The wadding combusted as it was set off, landed on the thatched roof, which promptly caught fire. Within two hours the entire structure burned to the ground."

"Good heavens," I exclaimed, remembering the theatre I had seen so recently, "the poor devils inside!"

"The 'poor devils' escaped, down to the last man, woman and child," Bryson reassured me, amused that I had become so involved in events that had taken place so long ago. "The only man even mildly discomfited was a nobleman whose britches caught fire and someone soon put that conflagration out with a bottle of ale. Whether his saviour was ever paid for the ale, history does not record."

He smiled a small smile and waited for the reaction he must have received from several generations of nervous undergraduates. When it was not forthcoming, he continued . . .
"So popular was the Globe with the populace

of London that it was rebuilt on the same spot and to an almost identical design within a year. Shakespeare chose that moment to retire to Stratford-upon-Avon. He cashed in his 'share', lived like a lord and died three years later in 1616. All of those marvellous achievements and when he died the man was a mere fifty-two years old!" He paused, as if the thought had just struck him.

Holmes chose the moment. "Rose," he said quietly.

The Professor responded like an actor being prompted.

"Oh, the Rose had long since vanished. It was a pity, really. Bankside should have had room for both of them. After all, there were other play-houses south of the Thames—like the Swan. But there was something special about the Rose . . ."

He paused in thought, then continued . . . "When Philip Henslowe built his Rose playhouse on Bankside in 1587, it was *the* place to go to 'hear a play'. For several years he had it all to himself. You see, Southwark was on the south bank, out of the jurisdiction of the City Fathers, who would have banned the actors out of hand for their immoral goings-on. But on Bankside everything went on—plays, bear-baiting, prostitution . . . I always think 'whoring' sounds so much better, don't you?

"Henslowe did a little of everything, by all accounts, and even though Burbage had had his

Theatre since 1576—well, who wanted to make the journey to smelly old Shoreditch? And Henslowe had two other powerful reasons to lure the crowds to the Rose. He had Christopher Marlowe to write many of his most successful plays and he had his son-in-law, Edward Alleyn to act in them—*Doctor Faustus*, *The Jew of Malta*, *Tamburlaine*. Powerful stuff! For a while it's believed he even had the young Will Shakespeare. At least two of Shakespeare's early plays were performed at the Rose before he took off, crossed the river and threw in his lot with the Burbages.

"Even that didn't worry Henslowe unduly. In 1592 he even partly rebuilt and enlarged the Rose. Then disaster struck. Marlowe was killed in a tavern brawl—some said murdered for political reasons—and in 1597 Alleyn retired. He had enough money but he wanted the kind of respectability that was denied mere actors—and still is, from what I hear. He founded a school, which became Dulwich College and turned himself into a gentleman. Then, as if that were not enough to cope with, the Burbages arrived with their Globe and set up shop just down the road with a far superior theatre. Henslowe knew when he was beaten. He had the Burbages' builder, Peter Streete, construct a theatre like the Globe. Optimistically, he called his new venture the Fortune and he took his fortune north of the river, leaving the game to the Globe. By 1603—

when the old Queen Elizabeth died—the Rose was to all intents and purposes deserted.

"Many people were saddened to see it go; a few were extremely bitter. The diehards admitted Shakespeare and Burbage were all very well but—they said—you should have seen Marlowe and Alleyn in their prime to know what *acting* was all about.

"What Henslowe felt was not recorded, though he left detailed accounts of his business dealings. He simply got on with his other ventures. He even tried another playhouse close by the second Globe. He called it the Hope—he was nothing if not an optimist, even down to the *names* of his theatres! But the era of the amphitheatre play-houses was over and so was Henslowe's. He died in 1616—the same year as Shakespeare. Alleyn lived on for another ten years. In the 1640s Cromwell's roundheads did what the City Fathers had long talked of doing. They tore all the playhouses down and that was that. The Golden Age was over—and that, gentlemen, is the story of the Globe and the Rose . . ."

"Perhaps not quite *all* the story, Professor," Holmes added thoughtfully. "I think I can tell you without breaking client confidentiality that there are forces at work that are prepared to take some-what dramatic measures to prevent the Globe ever opening—even at this late stage. Can you think of some connection that might involve the Rose?"

Bryson leaned back in his chair and steepled his fingers. "As to the relative historical importance of the two playhouses . . . the 'Rosers' versus the 'Globers', if you like. Personally, I find the argument futile. The Globe was clearly more significant. In many ways it was the cradle of modern theatre. Nonetheless, there has always been a faction that espouses the cause of the Rose and believes that any rebuilding should have used it as the model. Many of my colleagues share that view. Oxford, I need hardly add, is not called 'the home of lost causes' for nothing!

"The rebuilding of the Globe on a new site has aggravated the Rosers. Since no one knows for sure precisely where in that general area either the Rose or the Globe were actually situated—such extant drawings as exist are most imprecise—they claim to be concerned that Adler's new site may mean that he is building on top of the Rose itself. I myself put no credence in the claim. My examination of the evidence has it several yards further back from the river but I fear there are those who will do anything to publish a paper or stir up an arcane controversy . . . I remember . . ."

And that was pretty much the substance of it. After leaving Professor Bryson, Holmes and I took a turn through the Master's Garden. It was a wonderful morning, bright and warm, though much of the heat had gone out of the sun and,

141

while the foliage was still green, there was a hint of brown on the tips of some of the leaves. On a day like this in such a haven of peace it was easy to see what might tempt a man to retreat from the ugly, fast-moving world that existed outside the college walls and spend his life absorbed in the placid wisdom of the past. These reflections caused me to ask Holmes if he had never contemplated the academic life.

"The thought has been put to me on more than one occasion, old fellow, but the idea would be anathema to me. In any case, I carry my own private study with me here"—and he tapped his forehead—"and I can enter it and lock the door any time I wish, for it is stocked with all the furniture I am likely to use. No, to dwell within these halls would be to commit oneself to studying what *has* been and that is only part of the truth. I need to study what *will* be. Pope talked of the proper study of Mankind being Man and he was quite right. Walk down those teeming streets, peer into those crowded little houses, have your mind imprinted with that endless gallery of faces grim or gay . . . all of that is my meat and drink, Watson. It is the endless juxtapositions that appeal to me, the possibilities—but I am beginning to wax philosophical. I fear there must be something potent in the air here!

"Come now, Watson," he added, changing the subject that was beginning to embarrass him, "take a look at the steps of the Hall over there. What do you see and what do you observe?"

To indulge him I said: "I see a college servant sweeping the steps, I see an elderly man—clearly a don—descending them . . ." Then, deciding to score a point for myself—"I see *no* undergraduates, since they are all away on vacation until October . . . and finally, I see a young man in clerical garb who, by the way he is looking about him, does not belong to the college and is probably a tourist . . ."

"Excellent," said Holmes, "and the cleric. Is there anything familiar about him?"

I looked more closely. The man seemed to be examining architectural details in a fairly random manner, as though finding something to do to fill his time. That, however, was by no means a criminal offence. Other than that, there was nothing remarkable about him. Of middle height and slightly built, he wore a rather large brimmed hat that obscured much of his face and sported a large and extremely luxuriant moustache of the kind then in fashion. Though, come to think of it, I had not seen too many of them adorning ecclesiastical faces. I said as much to Holmes, then added: "But after all, who notices a vicar, once you've identified him *as* a vicar?"

"Precisely, Watson," said Holmes clapping me on the back almost painfully, *"precisely!* It is because your reactions are so normal that you are so eminently useful. The leaf in the forest. No one thinks to look at the individual leaf once the fact of there *being* leaves is taken for granted. The same is true of certain people. The curate and the cabbie have that in common. So does the postman. They fade into the wallpaper of our daily lives. Would it surprise you to know that the gentleman we have just been discussing—who I notice has just realised we are talking about him—shared the compartment with us from Paddington?"

"It most certainly would," I replied, realising I had once again failed one of Holmes's tests. Sensing that my feathers were beginning to be ruffled, he quickly went on—"Oh, don't let that upset you, old fellow. He wasn't a vicar then but a sober-suited businessman, also with a large and equally false set of facial hair. As an investigator, I should be of precious little use if I could not see through a disguise. What the amateur fails to realise is that it is far easier to change the outward appearance than it is to eliminate certain physical mannerisms of which one is often quite unaware. Our friend, for instance, has the habit of rubbing his right hand against the side of his face, as if brushing something away. See—he's doing it now." And, indeed, the "cleric", unsettled by our scrutiny, performed the gesture exactly as Holmes had described it.

"I fancy we shall have our friend's company on

the return journey. Someone is clearly taking no chances between now and tomorrow night of our slipping the net. We shall have to see what we can do about that. Well, Watson, if you have inhaled enough of the rarified Balliol air, I suggest we begin a quiet stroll towards the station. Let our watcher in the shadows see you take a good look at your watch, there's a good fellow. We want him to have plenty of time to anticipate our arrival. Good. There he goes . . ." And, indeed, the young man seemed to be filled with a new sense of purpose, as he turned and began to make for the lodge and the street beyond.

As we followed in more leisurely fashion, I turned to my friend—"Well, at least we know the meaning of the rose drawing but are we any nearer to knowing who's behind all this? I can understand that feelings might run high but surely . . ."

"No, there's more to this than some academic argument, Watson. More and, in a sense, less. Scholars love to wound one another with words but in general they are men of bile more than blood. No, the Rose is in every sense a stage on which our drama is being acted out but for *one* of our players it has taken on a greater symbolic meaning and it is that meaning that we must uncover. And quickly before some greater tragedy is enacted."

He was silent until we reached Oxford station, when the sight of the young cleric appeared to revive his spirits. As he had predicted, our shadow took a seat where he could observe us and overhear us, should we have been rash enough to say anything worth overhearing. As it was, the journey back to London must have frustrated him immensely. Much to Holmes's amusement I entered into the spirit of things and regaled him and our unfortunate travelling companions with a series of highly detailed tales of my military exploits in the Afghanistan campaign, including a searing account of how I had taken the Jezail bullet which still troubled me on damp days.

As we left the compartment at Paddington, Holmes lingered briefly by the seat occupied by the young man and I observed him whisper a few words into his ear. He rejoined me, smiling mischievously.

"What on earth did you say to him?" I asked.

"I merely gave it as my opinion that to achieve the look of an older man, Leichner's Number 6 grease stick is infinitely to be preferred to the Number 4."

"And what did he say?"

"Oh, I think Mr Phipps agrees with me entirely. He certainly didn't argue the point."

CHAPTER NINE

A nd so to London, my mind searching through the clues for the murderer's identity. And now we had it: "*Phipps!* Yes! Well, that settles things, surely. He must be our man?"

"Oh, Phipps is our man, certainly, but not *the* man. The second of the 'three'. As we saw in the death of Fiske, he is most certainly involved, though I would guess against his will. No, Watson, he is the puppet but someone else is pulling his strings. It's the puppet master I want and I mean to have him."

"Phipps, Dame Ivy and the mysterious A N Other, eh?"

"That's right. 'We three'. The clue was right there in the very first quotation we received from the 'paperboy' but I was too self-absorbed to see it. Perhaps you'll be kind enough to edit that fact from the account of this adventure that I feel sure you will write? You remember the line—'We three, to hear it and end it between them'? In my arrogance I assumed the writer was creating in his mind some sort of trinity between himself and the two of *us,* when what he meant—in *his* arrogance—was the three of *them*. He was laying down the gauntlet, challenging us to stop them. To do that, of course, we must first identify them."

"At least we've got two of them," I said encouragingly. "All we have to do now is find the murderer."

"Good old Watson," Holmes laughed as we descended from the cab that had brought us the short distance from Paddington and I turned to pay the cabbie. "It never fails to amaze me how well balanced we are. I invariably see the cup as almost empty, whereas you persist in seeing it as almost full! You are quite right, of course— we *are* making progress, if only by a process of elimination and we do have the ball of yarn in our hands that will lead us through the maze to the lair of the Minotaur. What we grievously lack is time. Which is why we must take a shortcut."

As we were in our room and hanging up our coats, he continued . . . "There is one basic flaw in the argument you were propounding just now. In all likelihood we do not have a murderer because we do not have a *murder* . . ."

"What on earth do you mean, Holmes?" I expostulated, "What about poor old Fiske?"

"Oh, Fiske was 'murdered' in every moral sense of the word, no doubt about that. The intention was clearly there. But in reality what killed Fiske was the abuse of his physical condition— encouraged by the 'murderer'—and the absence of the substance that would have been the antidote. Fiske in essence killed himself—with someone else holding his hand. I can hear a defence lawyer using those very arguments on behalf of whoever we put in the dock."

"Well, then, there was the attack on young Allan . . ."

"*Was* there? I wonder. You know my suspicions. In any case, that will never come to court. As she was leaving Mrs Adler informed me that Allan claims it was an accident and does not wish the police to investigate further. Under these circumstances that particular case is closed.

"No, old fellow, as far as the law is concerned or we can presently prove, our man has done nothing criminal. Frightening a young lady with a harmless snake is hardly a crime, even if his fingerprints were all over it in indelible ink!"

"But all the *notes* . . . ?"

"*Billets-doux* from one Shakespeare lover to another. Don't misunderstand me, Watson, the underlying intent is undoubtedly malicious but at this very moment the police are powerless. Until a genuine crime has been committed, by which time . . ." He did not need to complete the thought. We were both thinking of a certain lady.

It was Holmes who ended the reverie. "However," he said, "there is one thing we can completely sure of." He answered my look of interrogation by waving a hand towards the table. "We shall solve nothing if we ignore the inner man. It may have escaped your observation, Watson, that while our journey to Balliol provided us adequate food for thought, the good Professor did not think to offer us lunch. Luckily, Mrs Hudson has anticipated that eventuality. If you will be good enough to take the covers off those plates, I think you will find your favourite cold cuts.

"In any case," he added as we tucked in our napkins, "I seem to recall that Balliol cuisine has rarely matched its intellectual appetite."

That evening I had a long standing arrangement to attend a reunion of my old regiment. Under the circumstances I offered to put it off but Holmes would have none of it. "You go off and fight the good fight all over again," he said with a smile. "I only wish I could boast the camaraderie of a similar society but then, what would such a group be called—a detail of detectives? An inquiry of investigators? We should all be reading plots into a simple comment on the weather! I have certain administrative matters to attend to that would only tax your patience."

So off I went, squeezed into a dress uniform that had fitted me perfectly well for years until my wife's cooking had taken its toll, leaving Holmes furiously puffing an old briar, as he dashed off a series of notes and telegrams for young Billy to dispatch.

I have often observed that these occasions of bonhomie and reminiscence prove more taxing than many of the events being relived. And while I personally have total recall of those far off days, I find increasingly that many of my colleagues have very different recollections of the same events and in their accounts always seem to take the more heroic role.

We were well into the Afghan campaign and young Carruthers—who, come to think of it, can't be a day under fifty—had just defined our front line with a set of walnut shells, when a waiter murmured in my ear that I had a visitor waiting in the lobby. Ignoring the rowdy remonstrations of my fellows, I made my way there to find Holmes pacing to and fro.

"Sorry to interrupt the sacred ritual, Watson," he said, bundling me into my overcoat, which he had already retrieved, "but I'm sure you'll agree that murder takes precedence over Maiwand."

"*Murder?*" I said, desperately trying to focus my thoughts.

"Yes, and I'm afraid most foul. Come, there's not a moment to lose!" And not another word would he say until our cab pulled up outside a small residential hotel in a Bloomsbury back street.

Two police constables were keeping a firm eye on a small and mildly inquisitive crowd—being Bloomsbury, they were too well bred to show undue interest. Inside the musty and overdressed entrance hall a portly and equally overdressed proprietress was wringing chubby hands and repeating to Lestrade that nothing like this had ever happened in her establishment, indeed it hadn't, as if the Inspector had somehow suggested otherwise.

"Evening, gentlemen," said Lestrade, clearly relieved to see us. Then, taking in my apparel— "Glad to see somebody's enjoyed a good dinner this evening." Holmes was clearly in no mood for such jocularity. "Perhaps you will be so good as to show us where the body was found?"

Lestrade proceeded to lead us up a narrow staircase to the third floor and indicated a door where yet another constable stood guard. A moment later Holmes was inside what the establishment undoubtedly referred to as a suite but which was, in effect, little more than one large room with a kitchen alcove and a tiny bathroom opening off it. It was the bathroom that drew my friend's attention. Although someone had now turned the tap off, it was clear that at some point in the recent past water from the tub had overflowed. Tentacles of black reached into the green of the living room carpet.

"It was the water coming through the ceiling that alerted Mrs Harris here." It was Lestrade, now just behind us with the chubby proprietress straining to look over his shoulder. "We have a special sign in all the bathrooms about not letting the tub overflow," said that good lady primly.

"And I'm sure under normal circumstances she would have observed it most meticulously," said Holmes from the bathroom door. "Unfortunately, on this occasion I'm afraid she had very little say in the matter. This way, Watson, if you please. The final curtain of the late Dame Ivy Fosdyke . . ."

As I squeezed past Holmes, I was greeted by the kind of sight that never fails to remind me how tentative is our tenure on this planet. The bath was of the large old-fashioned variety. Above it and set into the wall was a shower head and around the bath was a shower rail to hold a curtain to contain the flow of water. Now the rail was buckled with just a few of the rings in place. The curtain itself had been torn free and now acted as a sort of improvised shroud for the figure lying in the bath.

Dame Ivy looked more angry than afraid as she faced her last audience. It was as though she felt some incompetent extra had given her her cue before she had arranged her costume properly. The "costume" was made of some sort of heavy material of the tarpaulin variety—originally an unattractive shade of green, now made even uglier by the bloodstained slashes that criss-crossed it.

"My God, Holmes, whoever killed her must have stabbed her at least a dozen times," I whispered, wishing that I now had the brandy that Holmes had interrupted. For all the times I've witnessed it, sudden violent death never fails to turn my stomach.

"Indeed, Watson, there is hysteria at work here, since any one of these blows would have been sufficient to dispatch someone so frail."

"I suppose we don't need to ask who . . . ?"

"No, I'm afraid that's all too obvious. And although he didn't choose to leave us the murder weapon as a present, he did leave us his calling card." And Holmes indicated the bathroom mirror behind me. There, finger painted in the lady's blood, were the words . . .

THOU WRETCHED, RASH INTRUDING
FOOL, FAREWELL.

and beneath them the crude drawing of a rose. "Hamlet to the dead Polonius when he's stabbed him through the curtain in his mother's room," Holmes mused. "Another Shakespearean method of death. And now 'we three' are two."

Lestrade had now joined us in the doorway and was doing his best to shield the inquisitive Mrs Harris from the contents of the room. "But why would our man kill *her,* Mr Holmes? According to your theory, they was on the same side, surely?"

"*Were,* Lestrade. 'Were' being the operative word. But the Rose Killer—as I'm beginning to think of him—sees treachery everywhere and plots in profusion. Perhaps he felt Dame Ivy was starting to lose her nerve . . ." I thought back to the scene by the gates of the Globe and could well believe that interpretation. "Perhaps, on the other hand, she was up to her old blackmailing tricks and pushed up the price of her loyalty. Either way, I'm afraid she got more than she bargained for."

"Well, Watson," turning to me, "there's nothing more we can do here and Lestrade seems to have his hands full . . ." And, indeed, as we left Lestrade was calling for the constable to help him with the recumbent Mrs Harris, who had managed to get a glimpse of her late guest and promptly fainted clean away.

As I followed my friend down the stairs, I heard him say to himself—"I am in blood stepped in so far that, should I wade no more, returning were as tedious as go o'er."

Shakespeare once again, of course, but I hadn't the heart to ask him the source. We made our way home in virtual silence and said our goodnights. We both had much on our minds.

I have to confess it was late morning before I put in an appearance in our sitting room to find Holmes enrobed in his favourite old dressing gown and looking remarkably cheerful, I thought.

He seemed to read my mind and my mood. "My dear fellow, it doesn't take a private investigator with the eye of the proverbial hawk and deductive powers as yet unmatched in his profession to tell that a cup of coffee would make the difference between life and death. I believe there may be one left in the pot. Business has been brisk this morning."

He didn't elucidate on the last point and I must admit I was preoccupied with the proffered coffee pot. He had in no way understated its recuperative properties. A few minutes later I felt strong enough to bring up the subject of the case. Holmes's expression grew serious.

"I'm very much afraid our friend has crossed his own personal Rubicon. What began as a rather malicious game has now turned deadly earnest, as he sees that, not only is Adler not to be bullied into capitulation but that he himself is in danger. Last night something in him clearly snapped. He feared Dame Ivy was about to give him away and yet, ironically, while he might have been unmasked, it would have been hard to accuse him of anything. The worst that could have happened would be that he could no longer pursue his plan—and to him, I suspect, that is everything. So he killed Dame Ivy . . . and by doing so, changed the rules of the game."

"In what way, Holmes?"

"In the first place, we are now pursuing a murderer not a prankster and in the second, I have determined that we shall no longer be hostage to events of his creation but devise our own final act—an act in which your own part will be crucial." I knew him too well to bother to ask precisely what that part might be. He would tell me in his own way and in his own good time.

But Holmes's mind had already moved on to other matters. "Tonight, for instance, I want you to go to Adler's dinner first to represent us both. I may be a little delayed, so you will make my apologies. The guests will naturally try to use my absence to pump you about the progress we are making on the case."

"But what shall I say?" It was one thing to act in Holmes's stead but quite another to have to speak for him.

"You will say that I have solved matters to my satisfaction and that an announcement is imminent."

"But is that true?"

"Not entirely but our man is not to know that and this will put him off balance for the time we need to finish weaving our net. Already he will feel it tightening around him."

Remembering the exploits I had been discussing the night before, I threw my shoulders smartly back, which immediately revealed itself to be a mistake. "You can count on me, Holmes."

"I know that, old fellow. You are the needle of my compass." His smile was momentarily boyish and the years rolled away. Then he was back to business. "Since last we spoke the odds have shortened in our favour. We have two new allies."

"And who might they be?" I asked puzzled.

"The first is under this cloth," Holmes replied.

He moved across the room towards a large rectangular object covered by a dust sheet. "Meet the Gentleman from Dulwich." And he whisked the cloth away to reveal a large oil portrait of a tall, austere man in noble regalia. Something in the eye suggested that he was enjoying the moment, almost as though he were acting the part of a gentleman. "Doctor John H. Watson, may I introduce Edward Alleyn, founder of Dulwich College, formerly gentleman actor with the Rose—otherwise known as Doctor Faustus, the Jew of Malta and Tamburlaine the Great, among his many other incarnations."

"*Alleyn?* So this is the fellow old Bryson was talking about yesterday?"

"Quite right, Watson. And as much a character in the story of the new Globe as any of the actors on that stage. Although Alleyn himself had left any stage before the first Globe was even built, someone considers himself bound to defend the reputation he feels was eclipsed and with it that of the theatre he graced for so long."

"But this is madness, Holmes!"

"I must say there are certain elements of dementia here that are concerning, if only because it is impossible to predict what may seem logical and eminently reasonable to the skewed mind. Which is why we must proceed with caution and seek to disconcert that mind until we can neutralise it. And with that in mind, let me introduce you to the second gentleman I have recruited to our cause. He is waiting in the hallway."

Holmes moved to the door and opened it, addressing someone who, for the moment, was out of my line of vision. "Do come in, Mr Adler—I'm sorry to have kept you waiting. I believe you have already met my colleague, Doctor Watson?"

"Adler?" I said before the young man entered the room.

"Perhaps I should have said 'Tallis'," said Holmes, closing the door behind them, "since that is the name he chooses to be known by."

"No, Adler will do just fine, Mr Holmes," the young man said, as he came over to shake me by the hand. "Doctor, I owe you an apology for my crass behaviour the other day in my father's office. I've already made my peace with Mr Holmes and now I'd like to do the same with you. You must have thought me—what's the English phrase?—a damn fool."

"I have seen displays of better manners in the young," I replied, I'm afraid rather pompously.

At this Holmes burst out laughing. "Well put, Watson. You really missed your calling. You should have been a school master ordering six of the best." This made me laugh in turn and with that the ice was broken.

"As you know, old fellow," Holmes continued, "I'm not known for my diplomatic skills." I could have argued the point but didn't. "But in the light of the facts as we now know them . . ." and here he gave me a warning glance that said he was referring to only *some* of the facts that we had discovered—"I felt it was right to try and untangle some of the strands that had no direct bearing on the case but threatened to confuse it. Florenz Adler's relationship with his son was one of those strands. So last evening, in your absence, I invited them here separately without telling either who they were to meet. However, what I told both of them was that we needed their help in solving the Globe affair . . ."

I nodded and at that point Tallis jumped to his feet. "Perhaps I might pick up the story here, Mr Holmes? When I said I'd been a fool, Doctor, I meant just that. I don't suppose my story's that uncommon but it's been none the less painful for that. You see, ever since I found out who he was—and for years my mother wouldn't discuss the matter—my father has fascinated me and at the same time repelled me. Here he was, this imaginative and wildly successful man and yet, if he knew I existed, he ignored the fact. Of course, I've found since that he'd tried to find me and failed. I worshiped and hated him at the same time and, of course, my mother's bitterness was a steady drip of poison in a young mind. For years these feelings of mine festered. It was wasted and negative emotion, I knew that but, like a lot of children of famous and successful parents, I seemed incapable of doing anything about it.

"Then I took up the law—we were living in England by that time—and soon after my mother died. It was round about the same time—about eighteen months ago—that I heard of my father's scheme to rebuild the Globe. In fact, it was already quite well along but he'd kept his name out of it until then for obvious reasons. He knew it would create a local furore and it indeed did. Then, when that consortium came to my firm for legal advice in their attempt to take the project over, I volunteered my services to advise them. It seemed nicely ironic at the time. This man had hurt me and now I would have the power to hurt him. He cared more for his damned theatre than he did for his own flesh and blood. *Now* he'd have to notice me. The funny thing was that the harder I tried—and I should have known that any kind of pressure would only drive him to further efforts—the less satisfaction I derived from the whole business.

"The silly thing is that I began to realise quite clearly that what he was doing was *worth* doing, that I should be helping him do it not hindering. And when I met the man and told him who he was dealing with—and saw the hurt in his eyes . . . well, Doctor, I realised . . ."

"Revenge is bitter fruit," I suggested.

"Poetically and aptly put, Watson," said Holmes softly.

"And that's literally where you and Mr Holmes came in," Tallis continued. "Of course, I was too proud and stubborn to admit it then, even to myself. After all, I *am* Florenz Adler's son." He smiled in self mockery. "But when Mr Holmes invited me over to ask for some advice . . . and then I found my father sitting here . . . well, I'm afraid we both made fools of ourselves in front of him." He turned to my friend. "I'd like to say this in front of Doctor Watson, because I'd never be able to say it to you if we were alone. We're eternally grateful to you, Mr Holmes—and I speak for Adler and Son."

"Thank you, Mr Adler or Tallis or . . . you really must make your mind up what we are to call you. You really can't expect two middle-aged men to remember all these confusing details." With his deft mock confusion he caused us all to laugh and lowered the emotional temperature but I knew his expressions well enough to know that what Tallis had said had pleased him mightily. There was a romantic streak not too far below the surface of Mr Sherlock Holmes.

As if becoming aware of it himself, he brought us back to business. "For this evening—may I call you Henry?—I want you to carry on in public as though nothing has changed. You are Henry Tallis and you represent the interests of those who wish to take over Florenz Adler's control of the Globe project. Tomorrow the story may be different but for tonight's meeting that is the part you will continue to play."

"But where does *Florenz* Adler fit into all this?" I asked.

"He, too, has his part but—I hope you will both indulge me in this—I wish each of you to know only what is required of him. In that way the drama I have devised may take its prearranged course. Let us call it 'improvisational drama' around a given theme. One day perhaps the theatre will take a lesson from life. Only the two of you—and, of course, your father, Henry— know that there *is* a theme and a play taking place of our devising.

"Watson, you may recall that when Professor Bryson was describing to us the staging of Elizabethan plays he mentioned that the actors of the period were never allowed to read the whole play before they performed it. Instead, they were given only their own lines and had no idea which of their fellow actors was to play what part or speak what lines. An interesting concept, which I now intend to revive. From now on the stage is set and we are all merely players.

"And now, Henry, if you would be kind enough to accompany Mr Alleyn safely back to Dulwich, I believe he has played his part for now?"

"Certainly, Mr Holmes. In fact, I kept the cab

waiting around the corner. Doctor, I shall see you both this evening. Or rather, you will see *the* old Henry Tallis. Please don't be surprised at my chameleon behaviour. And should you need anything, I shall be right there at your command."

"I hope I shan't be in commanding mood," I smiled as I shook his hand. "Personally, I'm looking forward to an excellent dinner. It's always a pleasure to dine at the Savoy." As Holmes helped Tallis take the portrait down the stairs, I couldn't help wonder whether I'd missed some of the implications of his last remark. What was I supposed to 'command'?

When Holmes returned, I was surprised at the gravity of his expression. "If nothing more positive comes out of this whole affair, my dear fellow, I feel the reconciliation of the Adlers will have been worthwhile." Then, seeing my expression, "Oh, I have few fears that we shall bring things to a satisfactory conclusion. But at what cost? At what cost?"

Then his expression changed and he was back in the present. Running his hand across his face, he smiled: "Watson, to see you looking so sleek makes me ashamed of my bedraggled appearance. Events have held me captive these last few hours, I'm afraid, but now I must effect some necessary repairs. I can hardly take a young lady for lunch looking like this . . ."

And before I could ask the obvious question, he

was out of the room, calling over his shoulder—
"Oh, and by the way, Watson, if you would be
so good as to meet me in the lobby of Brown's
Hotel at 3:00 p.m., there is someone I'd like you
to meet . . ."

CHAPTER TEN

Brown's Hotel is a small, cosy hotel that resembles the rather overgrown private home it presumably once was. It lies in smug seclusion in a Mayfair back street a short walk from the West End sights and for that reason, I suspect, has been the scene of many a clandestine tryst. It has always amused me to imagine agents of foreign powers slinking furtively in through the Street entrance, exchanging their secret documents and then leaving by the door to Albermarle Street.

In fact, the first person I spotted as I entered the vestibule could easily have qualified for my little scenario, had he not been talking to my friend Holmes. He was a small neatly dressed man, wearing a suit which looked to be of European cut. A short beard and rimless glasses added to the appearance. When he turned in my direction and spoke, the matter was beyond dispute. The accept was distinctly Middle European. "You I deduce are Doctor Watson, yes?"

It was Holmes who was the first to respond. "Forgive me, Watson, I was wool-gathering. May I introduce my good friend, Sigmund Freud?" Seeing the puzzlement on my face, he went on. "I had the pleasure of spending time with Doctor— soon, I believe, to be *Professor* Freud?" The little man inclined his head gravely. "As I say, we spent time together during my post-Reichenbach wanderings.

"Dr Freud has made a special study of the workings of the human mind, particularly in its less ordered conditions, and when I read in today's paper that the great man was visiting London . . ."

"Yes, I am to supervise the translation of my work into English. It is called *The Interpretation of Dreams*. It is not—as you would say—'a piece of cake.'

"Your language is insufficiently precise for my purposes."

Holmes chose to ignore this linguistic cavil. "So you see, Watson, I do read something besides the crime reports and the agony column," he smiled. "I contacted my friend immediately, sent him some background reading and asked him if he would spare us a few moments. As you see, he has been good enough to accept my invitation. Gentlemen, why don't we make ourselves comfortable in the lounge?"

Freud gave a precise little nod and we both followed Holmes into a small parlour-like room, where we made ourselves comfortable around a somewhat rickety table.

The good doctor opened his mouth as if to say something but Holmes raised a hand to prevent him. "Sigmund, I'm afraid you have the temporary advantage of Watson here and I am anxious he should be fully informed before you give us your expert opinion. Events unfolded somewhat briskly these past few hours and it seemed imperative to get the relevant papers into your hands with all dispatch. You have them with you?"

Freud produced several sheets of folded paper from an inside pocket and I could see at a glance they were more of the cablegrams we had received earlier. Without a word he passed them across to me.

"Perhaps you'll be good enough to glance through what Pinkertons have to say, Watson. They have been their usual effective selves and provided us with the missing piece of the puzzle. Unfortunately, what they have unearthed— especially in the light of last evening's events— gives more rather than less cause for concern."

The cablegram, which ran to several pages, was headed—"Re: Mrs Joan Lithgow."

"Who is 'Mrs Joan Lithgow'?" I looked up from the papers.

"Read on, Watson. All will become clear."

I did as he asked.

There was a covering note from the man Summers, stating that they had been unable to contact the final name on Holmes's list in person and it was believed that he had left the US, probably for England, some months ago. There followed details of the adoption of a male child through the Blackett Adoption Agency of Seattle by a Mr and Mrs Christopher Lowe in February 1866. Having remained in the Seattle area for many years, the family had moved to Canada where both the Lowes had been killed in a railway accident almost a year ago—at which point their son, who had lived with them throughout, had disappeared from the family home after settling their affairs. His name was Henry.

I couldn't refrain from interrupting my reading once more. "Henry Lowe? We haven't even *met* a Henry Lowe! What has all this to do with the Globe and someone trying to assassinate the Queen?"

"The human mind will often take a tortuous and tortured path to reach what it believes to be the light," Holmes replied, "and when that mind sees life through a distorted prism . . . But you will soon see what I mean."

I returned to my reading. Their investigations— Summers continued—had revealed the fact that the Lowes had another child, a daughter, also adopted. Her name was Joan, she was three years older than Henry and was now married to an engineer called Lithgow and living in San Francisco. She had been contacted and the letter that followed was her sworn deposition.

To Whom it May Concern:
I write this out of concern for my brother,

Henry Lowe. My parents adopted him when I was three years old. They had hoped for a child of their own and the doctors had told them that, after adopting a first child, a woman often conceives. In their case this was not to be but Henry—as they called the baby—gave them all the joy they could have wished for from their own child and I could not have wished for a more wonderful brother. From his earliest years he was full of fun and imagination. He would invent little plays in which I was always cast as the maiden in distress and he the hero who would rescue me from the wicked dragon or whatever. We were a very happy family.

It was my parents who sparked Henry's interest in the theatre and acting. There was no serious theatre within many miles of where we lived, so they formed their own little amateur group, which they called The Lowe Players and Henry, even as a very young boy, would make himself useful behind the scenes and sometimes in small parts.

Then, when he was about fifteen, he had an accident on his sledge one winter. It crashed into a tree and he suffered appalling head injuries. He was young, so he got over the physical aspects fairly quickly but he was never quite the same Henry in other ways. He would suffer from terrible headaches and there would be wild mood swings. One minute he would be on top of the world, the next he'd be in a black depression. The doctors said he'd probably grow out of it and all we could do was hope they were right.

The drama group seemed as though it might be his salvation. He threw himself into it more and more and became a very fair actor. He began to study the history of the theatre and he'd buy up old second-hand books, beg and borrow them from anywhere.

Then one day he took me aside and said he'd made a great discovery and that he had to tell me but I mustn't share it with anyone else. He made me swear on the Bible. At first I thought it was a big joke but he was so intense that I began to feel curiously frightened. Then he showed me this old book about Elizabethan theatres. Of course, it meant nothing to me. All I could see on the page he marked was an old drawing of a round wooden building without a proper roof. When I said as much, he got really angry. "Don't you see?" he cried. "Look at the *name* in the caption underneath!" So I did. It said

"Henslowe's Rose". I still didn't understand. He seized me by the shoulders and began to shake me. "The *line*," he said, "it wasn't broken after all. *We're* the continuation of the line. Henry . . . Lowe . . . Hens-lowe." At first I thought he was joking, then I realised he was in deadly earnest. A pulse was beating in his forehead and he kept putting his hand up to it. By this time the anger had passed and I got him to sit down quietly, as I tried to explain that it was just a coincidence. Lowe wasn't even our real name for either of us. We were adopted and we'd never been told what our real names were.

That seemed to make him sad for a while, then he said—"But that's just it. It's a reincarnation. It was all *meant*." Then a puzzled look came over his face. "Perhaps *I'm* the one and Mom and Dad aren't supposed to know. We mustn't tell them— it may affect the line of Destiny."

To cut a long story short, he made me promise to keep the secret which wasn't difficult—for what could I have told them that wouldn't have worried them sick? But I must say the secret seemed to please him and to an extent, calm him. Every now and then he'd come and tell me of another discovery from his "research".

"You know Dad's name is Christopher?" he said one day. "Well, who do you think was Henslowe's main playwright? Christopher *Mar-lowe*. And he was mysteriously killed in a fight in a tavern. They were out to get us even then."

He would go on like this and one day I asked him who "they" were. Then he told me how Henslowe and his Rose theatre were finally put out of business by the people who built another theatre nearby. The Globe, I think it was, and they had Shakespeare writing all these great plays for it. When he got to this part, Henry would get very excited and start saying that he—Shakespeare—had been "theirs", the Rose's, until the plot began. He seemed to have learned every word the man ever wrote off by heart—at least, that's the way it seemed to me.

I'm making him sound as if he was really weird all the time but that's wrong. Mostly, he was the same sweet boy I'd grown up with. It was just this one subject and it seemed to be like a lightning conductor for all the bad feelings, so I was glad in a way and even got used to it. And, as I say, our parents never knew anything.

Then the time came when I got married and moved away. I wasn't too worried about Henry by then. He seemed so much better. Clay, my husband, and I started a family of our own and time went by. Henry got an office job but most of his spare time went into the acting group and we kept in touch. I'd almost forgotten about what I used to think of as "Henry's Dream" and I supposed he had, too. Perhaps he had.

One day about a year ago I got the dreadful message that our folks were dead—both of them, just like that. I came back for the funeral, of course, but Henry had arranged everything. There was so much to do that there wasn't time for much private conversation and, in any case, I had Clay and my two little ones with me. But as we left the graveside, Henry said a strange thing to me. He said—"Don't worry, I'll take care of it. The Rose will be avenged." I didn't have the occasion to question him on what he meant by that and the next day we had to leave.

And that's the last I've seen of him. I had a note from the solicitors a few weeks later telling me what I'd been left in the will. Apparently, Henry had instructed them to put the family house on the market and I was to have the proceeds. He wanted nothing. He told them he had some very old unfinished family business to attend to and he left the town the very next day.

He's in my mind often and I wonder how he is. Henry is a good man but he needs help. I just hope he finds a friend who will lead him to peace of mind.

And there Joan Lithgow's letter ended. There was a postscript from Summers informing Holmes that a few days after Henry Lowe's departure, there had been a report of a break in at the offices of the Blackett Adoption Agency. Only the historical files had been disturbed and it was not yet known if any were missing.

I handed the papers back to Holmes. "I'd be prepared to bet a pound to a penny that the only one they *won't* find will be marked 'Charlotte Mencken'."

"For once, Watson, that's not a bet I'd take. I think we can safely assume that Henry Lowe, in his determination to trace his antecedents, found enough evidence in that simple folder to set him on a trail which led him from Charlotte Mencken to Carlotta Adler to the man who married her, Florenz Adler, who just happens to be rebuilding the playhouse that destroyed the Rose. A skein of happenstance that will have all the inevitability of Greek—or, more aptly, Shakespearean— tragedy to his soured mind . . ."

"*Hamlet.*" This from Freud, more of a statement than a question.

"Hamlet, indeed," Holmes replied, "which is why our friend Mr Allan was so anxious to play the part that he laid siege to Adler the moment he got off the boat. In doing so, he immediately began to create a situation in which confusion would become more confounded."

"Ah, so . . ." Freud picked up the thread. "I doubt very much that he realises Adler *is* his natural father. Indeed, if he even suspects it, his ego will be fighting it. He is fixated on Carlotta Adler, the woman he knows to be his mother. But in his fantasy he has also equated her with Gertrude, who, he believes, is betraying his unknown but presumably dead and certainly heroic father with Adler, the Claudius figure. In one way or another both must be punished for the sins of omission and commission. Yet to punish his mother recreates the Oedipus myth and leads to unbearable sin. The man is being torn apart by the Furies. He needs to invent nothing more. Shakespeare has already written the text for him.

"The man is hopelessly torn. Like many children, he probably fantasised about being a foundling. His parents weren't his real parents— something which, in due course, he found to be true, thus giving greater credibility to the rest of his imaginings. By that time, however, he was locked into another parallel fantasy. He was the reincarnation of Rose and its protagonists. With no one qualified to advise him . . ." He coughed modestly—"something like this was almost certain to happen. The *real* Allan—if I may call him so—wishes no one any real harm. He merely wishes to upset Adler's plans and so rebuke his mother. But the dark side of him cries out for Revenge!" Here he almost leapt to his feet, so convinced was he by his own rhetoric. "It is a question of which side will prevail. I find it a most interesting case."

"Ted Allan, eh?" I mused aloud. "Had my eye on him from the beginning." Holmes's quizzical expression caused me to change the subject hurriedly into a question—"But why did he choose that particular name? No one would have recognised him if he'd kept his own name . . ."

Freud was now clearly into one of his favourite subjects. Putting his fingers together—perhaps in unconscious emulation of the way Holmes himself was now sitting—his voice took on the tone of the lecture room.

"Quite simple, given what we know. His dementia is undergoing a classic metamorphosis. As I say, he now identifies totally with the story of the Rose, as he knows it, and with its 'characters'. But, if I am not mistaken, there are *two* characters who were equally key to that story. Henry Lowe has already turned himself into Henslowe. So what does the name 'Ted Allan' suggest to us?"

He scanned our faces as if we were one of his seminars . . . Suddenly I found myself saying—

"Ed . . . *Edward* . . . Allan . . . good God—Edward *Alleyn* the Rose's great actor!"

"Correct. Henslowe is also becoming Alleyn. You must understand that, as the mood takes him, both men also inhabit his mind. And not even he is to know which one will be in the ascendant or when."

"So the man is effectively a split personality?" said Holmes, sucking the stem of his pipe thoughtfully.

"Exactly so. Dementia Praecox . . . Schizophrenia . . . call it what you will. There was a most interesting case brought to my attention recently in Prague of a station master who . . ."

We were not to hear of the station master's problems for Holmes had jumped to his feet and was pacing the room.

"The good doctor, I'm afraid, confirms my own reading of the signs. Much as we might like to share Mrs Lithgow's optimism about her brother's prognosis, recent events dictate a more sinister interpretation—and since we have *two* Queens to protect, we must distract him from whatever bizarre scheme he has devised. So far he has largely had things his own way but tonight he will learn that, despite all he has done, he has still failed to dissuade Adler from opening his theatre."

"Why," I said, "surely that will shock him back to some form of reality? And in any case, last night's business . . ." I didn't want to say too much in front of Freud but I need hardly have worried. He was lost in his own world of theories and speculations.

"In the ordinary way I'd agree with you, Watson," Holmes replied. "Lestrade and his men are pursuing their enquiries, as they quaintly put it. He was round to see me this morning before you made your appearance. It appears the hotel has a large transient population and the redoubtable Mrs Harris makes a point, she assures him, of treating her guests as members of the family letting them come and go as and when they please. In short, the door is always on the latch and anyone can take the chance of entering. Our friend Allan clearly took that chance and got away with it. Oh, I don't doubt Lestrade will turn up something in time—but time is the one thing we do not have between now and Tuesday's royal opening. We must seize events before we become their victim."

Freud had apparently come to some further conclusion he wished to impart.

"May I add something?" said the doctor. "You taught me much during our 'sabbatical', Mr Holmes. I have learned to pay such attention to coat sleeves and collars that many of my patients become nervous. Perhaps I am even causing trauma they did not have in the first place—I jest, of course. But if *I* may offer *you* a piece of advice . . . However unbalanced his version of things appears to you—and I admit to you that I found it hard to read his sister's account unmoved—to him what he is doing is perfectly logical. He is pursuing a holy cause every bit as much as one of your . . ."

"Crusaders?" I offered.

"Crusaders, exactly. Dr Watson's hope may be realised, though my experience of such cases causes me to doubt it. I fear he is too far over the edge and must go forward or betray the cause. As for his three faces . . . In my country we have a kind of clock where little human figures come in and out of a house to indicate the weather. Allan . . . Lowe . . . Allan . . . Lowe . . . in and out . . . in and out. And then, of course, we must not forget the young man who was there to begin with. Though he, I fear, we shall see less and less. None of them responsible for the thoughts or actions of the others. None of them necessarily *aware* that the others exist."

Ever the practical man, I asked the obvious question—"So what do you suggest, Doctor?"

"Ah!" Freud was not to be caught so easily. "Solutions are not my business. I merely seek to understand and clarify the problems for my patients. But I tell you this, Mr Holmes, you will not reach this poor young man by your usual stratagems. You must seek him in the theatre of the mind."

And he sat back and folded his hands in front of him, as though the case were already solved. Then a thought struck him and he pulled out of a waistcoat pocket a large watch of the kind my father called a turnip and consulted it earnestly.

"I have another appointment, gentlemen. You will excuse me?"

"Of course, Doctor," said Holmes. "In any case, Watson and I must be on our way. There is much to be done."

As Freud rose, he pulled another document from his pocket and began to study it. "Now that you have had the benefit of my advice—to which you are more than welcome," he added quickly, realising that he had perhaps sounded churlish— "perhaps I may ask your advice on a somewhat intractable matter?"

"Certainly," Holmes and I spoke almost in unison.

"Last night, my friend, I took your suggestion to visit the Oxford . . ."

"*Oxford?*" I said. "Why Holmes and I were there only the other . . ."

"No, no," Freud interrupted irritably. "Not Oxford. The Oxford Music Hall of which your friend speaks so highly. To see Mr George Robey . . ." and he consulted what I could now see was a theatre programme. "What means—'The

181

Prime Minister of Mirth'? I did not know there was such an office. For what is it responsible?"

For once I saw my friend nonplussed. "For public morale," was the best he could offer. To help him, I suggested—"Didn't you find his humour rather—local?"

"Oh, it was not Herr Robey who interested me," he replied. "I have long ago given up your English humour as impenetrable. No, it is the *audience* which find such a man amusing that I wished to study."

"And what were your findings?" I was foolish enough to ask.

"I think the British have many problems." And with a brief fusillade of handshakes, he was gone.

I turned from watching this remarkable man depart to find Holmes slumped back in the well-worn upholstery of his armchair, his fingers tented in front of his face—a piece of body language I knew denoted intense concentration. Nonetheless, I felt compelled to say what was on my mind.

"Surely in the light of this you must call the whole thing off and have Allan arrested?"

"On what grounds, pray?" Holmes was speaking into the middle distance. "We are morally certain that he is responsible for the death of two people and is prepared—there can no longer be any doubt of his intent or ability—to contemplate at least one more. Despite that, any competent lawyer would have him out on bail within hours, forcing him to go underground.

"Don't forget what Sigmund said, Watson. This man is more than one personality. Block one and you release another. Are they all guilty—or just the one? No, we need friend Allan in plain sight for the next little while, not lurking somewhere in the shadows, ready to strike. I am now totally convinced that I must put my plan into practice, though I had hoped to avoid it."

"What plan?" I asked.

Holmes continued as though I had not spoken. "There's a part for you in it, my old friend, as there always is, and I must ask you to stick to it to the letter—no matter what happens."

"You can count on me, Holmes," I said gruffly.

"I know that," he said rising to his feet and clapping me on the shoulder. "How many of my strategems have been built on this rock!"

As we left the hotel a thought seemed to strike him. "You know, Watson, Mr Shakespeare really is a remarkable fellow."

"I've never doubted it but in what way do you mean?"

"Just when you think you know what he means, life peels away another layer and reveals a new meaning in his words. Take the quotation about 'we three' . . . How blind I've been! First I thought he meant the three of *us* . . . then I thought he meant the three of *them*—himself and his accomplices. Yet in reality—and whether he's even conscious of it himself, I doubt he's referring to the three of *him*. The three personalities fighting within him. How many of them shall we meet before this is over, I wonder?"

Although the sun warmed my face as we stood looking for a cab, I felt as though someone had just opened a door at my back and let in a draught of cold air.

CHAPTER ELEVEN

It was one of those evenings we so rarely enjoy in London these days but which I seem to remember being so commonplace in my youth. The air was warm and still and the moon sent silver ribbons along the surface of the Thames as my cab drove along the Embankment. Because I had a little time to spare, I had asked the cabbie to take the longer route, so that I could enjoy the view. If I'm honest, I think I also wanted to give myself longer to prepare for the evening ahead.

Holmes, I felt, had been almost offhand as I left. Ever since we left Brown's I had sensed him retreat further within himself. It was a pattern I had become familiar with over the years, as a case reached a critical stage. It was as though he was husbanding his resources for the final throw and felt that any unnecessary word of action would only serve to dilute his energies.

As I was putting the final touches to my evening toilet and consulting my watch—I'm afraid army life makes one a stickler for punctuality—he emerged from his room, clearly far from ready.

"Watson, be a good fellow and go ahead, will you? It would be discourteous if we were both late. Apologise for my tardiness. I shall join you all later." Naturally, I agreed. Holmes could be somewhat unpredictable on social occasions. As I had my hand on the door knob, however, he said something that surprised and—the more I thought about it—concerned me. "Oh, and by the way, you would oblige me if you were to take your service revolver along." Before I could question him, I heard his door quietly close.

By the time the river came into view I had got over any irritation I might have felt. In any case, the beauty of London never fails to lift my spirits and tonight she was at her most radiant. Even now I could observe a host of little boats were busy plying their various trades up and down Old Father Thames and in my mind's eye—even though it was too far down river for me to see it, I could envisage the Globe standing proud and expectant as it looked across at the steps of Wren's mighty St Paul's. What would the next two days hold, I asked myself as the cab pulled up at the riverside entrance to the Savoy?

As the page showed me up to Adler's second floor suite with its river view, I found myself entering with Henry Tallis. It was only by the merest flicker of his eyes that I recognised my co-conspirator, Henry Adler. Seeing him and mentally adjusting to the role I had been assigned for the evening ahead, triggered off a parallel thought. Here was I, someone who never knowingly thought of the Bard from one year to the next, unable to get the fellow out of my head.

I kept thinking of the line about one man in his time playing many parts. Was there anyone in the room we were just about to enter who was really what they seemed on the surface? But then I reflected that they were, after all, actors. Perhaps this was their normal *modus vivendi*, merely complicated by a little matter of murder?

Tallis was as good as his word and proving to be a match for any of the professional actors in the room. The supercilious expression was never far from his lips as he circulated and I caught snatches of . . . "You say *when* the Globe opens. I should have thought it was a question of *if* the Globe opens . . ." For his part, Adler played the diplomatic host, choosing to ignore the obvious provocation. It was as though the two men had picked up the scene where they had left it in Adler's office. If I hadn't known better, I would have sworn the thing that concerned him most was to ensure that everyone's glass was full.

Over by the window Harry Trent was deep in conversation with Ted Allan. I went over to join them. Allan was none the worse for his "accident", he claimed, though I noticed that every now and then, when he was fairly sure that someone was noticing, he would unostentatiously put a hand to his side and allow his lips to tighten briefly. I felt inclined to advise him to practice the role of the invalid a little more before he took it on stage. At one point I fancy he interpreted my expression, because he changed the topic of conversation rapidly. "Mr Holmes will be joining us, will he not, Doctor Watson? I'm longing to be able to tell the folks back home that I actually sat at dinner with the famous detective."

I murmured something about my friend being detained on some important Government business but that he had assured me he would be along presently. At that moment Simon Phipps joined the group. Tonight he looked rather less ironed and polished than usual and the aphorisms didn't appear to be flowing. When there was a gap in the conversation and with the advantage of a second whisky and soda, I couldn't resist mentioning that Holmes and I had recently spent a most pleasant day in Oxford. "Do you know Oxford at all, Mr Phipps?" I asked. He mumbled that he was afraid he didn't, no. "Perhaps not the best time of the year to see it in some ways," I went on, the bit between my teeth. "Hardly a student to be seen. The place seemed to be full of vicars." And I found myself laughing loudly at my own joke.

There was an undertone of suppressed hysteria in every conversation that took the form of overly loud voices and excessive laughter. It was as though no one wanted to be the first to bring up the topic that was on everyone's mind—the death of Dame Ivy.

Suddenly there was one of those silences that sometimes occur during a party where there is no real chemistry between the guests and the first rush of conversation has been exhausted. With his sense of theatre Adler filled it superbly.

"First of all, let me thank all of you for giving up your time to be here but there are matters that affect us all which must be discussed openly. Second, let me be the one to mention what I know is on all our minds. The theatre has lost two of its most revered actors and we have lost two dear colleagues and friends . . ."

Knowing what I did, I couldn't help but feel that he was somewhat overstating the case. Nonetheless, he did it with total apparent sincerity. "The police assure me that everything possible is being done to bring the perpetrators of these appalling crimes to book but they can promise no immediate result. As a result, nothing has essentially changed since we last spoke. It is up to us to decide on our future course of action. But before we do, let us raise a glass to—'Absent Friends' . . ."

So saying, he proceeded to match the action to the word and there was another awkward moment as we all responded to one degree or another. I would have given a great deal to have been able to read the private thoughts in that room.

Then Adler continued—"I think we're all here, except for Mr Holmes, who has sent his apologies via Doctor Watson and will be with us shortly."

Carlotta whispered in his ear. "Oh no, I'm sorry we do have *one* absentee—the lovely Miss

French. However, since one of the few people in the world who scares me is the Savoy chef, I suggest we be seated. You'll find place cards by your seats."

And so the meal began and, while it wasn't a group that would ordinarily have made for an ideal social gathering, the drinks and Adler's words had softened the edge of understandable nervousness and general conversation flowed smoothly enough. Trying to think as Holmes would, I covertly surveyed the table.

On my right was Carlotta Adler, smiling brilliantly like the trained performer she was. As she questioned me about my wife's taste in opera—I had been foolish enough to offer up the subject to fill in a conversational lull but it served as well as anything—an anxious look would occasionally cross her face. In turn, I tried to convey reassurance that her secret was safe with me, though I doubt my acting skills were adequate for the purpose.

She was on firmer ground when she turned her attention to Harry Trent on her right. On the few occasions I had seen him I had noticed nothing to shake the impression of stolid, well meaning predictability. There was the same country boy courtesy about him tonight with a polite "Ma'am" for the ladies and a "Sir" for the two men—Adler and myself—who were his seniors. But would the colour in his complexion that was rising as the drink took effect show us another side of Mr Trent as the evening wore on?

Ted Allan on his right had apparently spotted the same signs as I had and at one point laid a restraining hand on Trent's arm, as if to discourage him from raising his glass—only to have it shaken off angrily. As far as I could tell, I was the only one to witness the incident. Allan appeared no more comfortable with his other neighbour, Simon Phipps, who seemed to have little appetite for the excellent *Sole Walewska* the chef had provided. Instead, he was draining his glass at regular intervals and on one occasion held it up peremptorily for the waiter to refill it. As he did so, I noticed that his finger nails were badly bitten, a feature at odds with the elegant appearance he had been at pains to present at our first meeting. I made a mental note to report that fact to Holmes. How often has he not lectured me on the significance of detail? The man's nerve was unravelling. Phipps's lapse earned him a muttered reprimand from Allan. On the surface, a friend concerned to prevent a friend from letting himself down in public. In reality, a general losing command of his troops. It was not proving to be a relaxing evening for Mr Allan.

Phipps perhaps had some excuse in that next to him was the empty chair set aside for Pauline French's arrival. As we were now well into the main course, it began to look increasingly likely that she would not be coming. On the other hand, this was not by its nature a casual invitation and one would have expected at least a note of regret.

On the other side of the gap and at the head of the table was Adler, of course. Knowing as I did, the game within the game—or, at least, the rudiments of it, I was fascinated by his performance. The concerned host, jovial at one moment, sincere and attentive to his guests the next, he managed to make everyone feel they were the sole object of his attention. Even now that people were seated and the noise around the table was rising as everyone competed to be heard, he somehow managed to catch enough of each separate conversation to be able to contribute. The man missed nothing and once again, I was forced to own a grudging admiration for him, having some knowledge of the pressures weighing upon him. From time to time out of the corner of my eye I was aware of his glance towards Henry Tallis, when he thought himself unobserved.

Tallis himself, kept up his end of a conversation with me about such uncontroversial topics as the situation in South Africa (worsening) and the political scene (which never appears to improve, whichever party happens to be in power).

This, then, was the happy band of pilgrims breaking Florenz Adler's bread and *Sole Walewska* that Sunday evening of September 17th, 1899.

It was Phipps who broke the thin veneer of

pretended normality. Draining his glass, he put it down on the table with an audible crash and rose unsteadily to his feet, leaning across Pauline French's empty place towards Adler. "Well, Mr Impresario Adler, when are you going to tell us what you intend to do? All of this is just a facade—I mean charade, isn't it? You'll decide what you want, no matter what we say, won't you?"

There was complete silence round the table. Then Adler rose to his feet. Whether he was setting out to act "Florenz Adler", it was difficult to tell but he cut an impressive figure with his napkin bunched in one hand and an unlit cigar in the other—so impressive that Phipps immediately subsided into his seat.

His eyes passed dismissively over Phipps and took in the rest of the table. "You're quite right, Simon. I *shall* decide. As they say in my country—'Money talks'. But *my* money has no intention of talking until it hears from all of you. So, since you were so anxious to speak, let's hear from you first. What do *you* think we should do?"

In my medical experience I have frequently noticed that inebriation can be temporarily arrested by a sudden shock and that is precisely what I saw happen to Phipps. He had been deliberately trying to drink himself into a state of oblivion until Adler had called his bluff. Now I fancied I saw a range of emotions pass across his face as he sat slumped in his chair. Unless I had lost any ability to judge another human being, this was a man who was not evil but lost. He seemed about to speak when, sitting immediately opposite him as I was, I saw something that none of the others except perhaps Carlotta Adler was in a position to see—I saw Ted Allan pull at the back of his jacket. In a voice that could barely be heard Simon Phipps, if that was indeed his real name, said—"I vote 'No'."

Adler looked at him for a moment to let the words sink in, then he raised his eyes to meet the rest of us. "Thank you, Mr Phipps. We have one 'No'. Mr Allan . . . ?"

A clear but quiet "No". No explanation was offered and the look he directed over Adler's right shoulder was devoid of expression.

"Mr Trent?"

All eyes turned to Trent and I would have lost the rest of my pension if I had bet on the answer. Trent drew himself to his feet and almost stood to attention as he said with that mid-Western drawl that I had supposed to be at least partly affected. "Mr Adler, when he died my father hated your guts and, as I stand here right now, for that self-same reason I hate your guts, too, but what you are doing is what *he* would have done. One of these days you and I are going to have a reckoning but on this issue—I say 'Yes', we go ahead."

Around the table I could hear the sound of

194

breath being slowly expelled and I realised that I had been holding mine, too—so much so that I barely heard Carlotta murmur: "My heart says 'No' but I'll back you in whatever you decide to do, you know that, Flo. May I please abstain?"

The look between Adler and his wife was beyond my powers to describe. Then he scanned the table once more. "By my reckoning that makes it one for, two against. Doctor, you'll excuse me if I leave you out of the reckoning but since we're involving interested parties, I think it's only fair if we let Mr Tallis have a say for the home team, so to speak. Though I guess we know how he'll vote, don't we? Mr Tallis, should we pull up sticks or should we go ahead?"

People talk about the silence of the tomb and until that moment I had always thought of it as one of those phrases used by writers of popular fiction. Then Tallis raised his eyes from the napkin that had been riveting his attention. "Well, if somebody's going to do it, I suppose it might as well be you. I vote 'Yes'."

The ripple of sound around the table was greater than such a small group should be able to generate. When it had died down, Adler said to no one in particular—"By my reckoning we have two 'Yeses' and two 'Nos'. And since those who are not with us cannot vote, that leaves the casting vote with me. It will hardly surprise you to hear that I vote that we continue. On Tuesday the show goes on. Mr Shakespeare has waited long enough. End of discussion. Now I suggest we . . ."

We never heard what he was about to suggest, for at that moment the door of the suite opened to admit a waiter carrying a silver salver. For no reason I could account for except the artificially charged atmosphere, every eye followed his progress as he crossed behind Carlotta and myself and approached Adler's chair. All conversation ceased as he presented the tray to the impresario. On it we could see a single folded piece of paper. Slowly Adler picked it up, unfolded and read it. His face was a mask as he looked across the table at me.

"Doctor Watson," he said, "in your colleague's absence, I think you had better look at this."

In a moment I was by his side and snatching the note from his hand. There at the bottom was the familiar drawing of a rose and above it the legend . . .

TOO MUCH OF WATER HAST THOU, POOR OPHELIA, AND THEREFORE I FORBID MY TEARS.

Hamlet

Without realising it, I found I'd been reading the words aloud. As if in answer, there was a shout from the other side of the table. Simon Phipps, white and trembling, had risen to his feet, knocking over his chair as he did so. Shock had dispersed the fumes of the drink, as it so often can.

"That's *my* speech," he cried . . . "it's Laertes' speech to his sister, Ophelia . . . to her body . . . after she's drowned!"

There was a moment while that sank in. Then Adler looked up at me. "And *Pauline* is to be our Ophelia—and she isn't here."

I was seized with a sudden dread intuition. It had to do with the peaceful river I'd been admiring on my way to the dinner, its surface sparkling with light and colour. Now through the window it was dark and threatening. I could imagine it reaching out hungrily for the body of a young woman whose only sin was to find herself accidentally caught up in the machinations of a deranged mind. The vision was all too real and at that moment I knew what had to be done— what Holmes would have done, had he been here.

"Adler," I said, "you'd better come with me. You, too, Tallis."

"Where to, Doctor?"

"Why, to the Globe, of course. And the river that runs by it . . ."

CHAPTER TWELVE

The bobbing lights of lanterns reflected from black water realised my worst fears. I have noticed in the past how at times of particular stress small details imprint themselves on the brain. I found myself staring at the plumes of steam rising from the flanks and nostrils of the cab horse that had rushed the three of us here. As the vehicle came to a shuddering halt in the lee of the dark playhouse, we scrambled out and rushed across the river walk to the steps of the temporary jetty that had been erected to receive Her Majesty's barge for Tuesday's gala opening.

A group of dark figures appeared to be bending over a white bundle that was lying on the decking. As we drew nearer, I heard a familiar voice urging the others to be careful. "Lestrade?" I cried. "That you, Doctor Watson?" the answer came back. "You're a regular godsend, Doctor, and no mistake. Here, boys, make room for the Doctor . . ."

With Adler father and son close behind me I made my way through what I now saw to be a half dozen or so uniformed policemen. I dropped to my knees beside the sodden white bundle I'd seen from above. It was a woman wearing a diaphanous white dress bizarrely woven with strands of artificial flowers. Someone had put a police uniform jacket under her averted head to act as a pillow but a pool of water was slowly forming around the poor creature. It was obvious that she had been pulled from the river only moments before we arrived. Not only was her face turned away from me but her long black hair—also garlanded with the same flowers—was pasted to the part of it that was visible. Gently I took her chin in my hand and turned her head towards me, combing back her hair with the fingers of my other hand.

As I had feared, I found myself looking at the beautiful impassive face of Pauline French. But, thank God, we were not too late. Her eyes flickered and opened, then gradually focused on me. "Doctor Watson?" she whispered, "how did you . . . ?" Then a look of terror crossed her face and she cried out—"Don't let them . . ." I patted her hand to reassure her. "Don't you worry, my dear. Whoever they are, they can't hurt you now." This seemed to calm her and her eyes closed.

A cursory examination told me that she was in no immediate danger and, rising to my feet, I turned to Lestrade and the Adlers. "Have a couple of your men use our cab and take her to the hospital as soon as possible. I don't think she's come to any real harm but we can't afford to take any chances. She doesn't appear to have been in the water long or her skin would show more signs of it. Adler, you must have something in your costume department they can wrap her in. She mustn't be allowed to catch cold."

Adler was a man who knew how to take instructions as well as how to give them. With a nod, he and Tallis hurried off to the Globe's stage door. While Lestrade's men were carefully carrying Pauline French up the jetty steps, I pulled Lestrade away from the crowd, so that we could talk without being overheard.

"How on earth did you happen to find her, Lestrade? Thank heaven you did. Even though it's not a particularly cold evening, she wouldn't have lasted long in that water wearing that flimsy dress."

"I wish I could say it was brilliant detective work on our part, Doctor," he answered through the gloom, "but that wouldn't be true. Since this whole Shakespeare business started, I've had two or three men patrolling the area around the theatre, just to be on the safe side, like. As they were due to change shifts, I thought I'd pop along and check up on things. I'd just arrived with the new fellows when we heard a splash and a woman's scream. Naturally, we all rushed over to the river wall and there, just down by the jetty, we could see this—ghost, it seemed like—floating there. It gave me a fair turn, I can tell you, Doctor. The water had spread her dress out all round her and it looked like somebody had thrown all these flowers over her . . ."

When down her weedy trophies and
herself
Fell in the weeping brook. Her clothes
spread wide,
And mermaid-like awhile they bore her
up . . .
. . . but long it could not be
Till that her garments, heavy with their
drink,
Pull'd the poor wretch from her
melodious lay
To muddy death.

We turned to find Allan, Phipps and Carlotta standing behind us. On the road above our heads the presence of another two cabs told how they had got here. It was Allan who had spoken the lines describing Ophelia's death.

Even though I was the only one whose clothes were the worse for the evening's events—I had been forced to kneel in the water on the deck— we were a bedraggled bunch compared to the elegantly dressed dinner guests of an hour or so earlier. It was as though the near tragedy had ruffled everyone's feathers. It was hard to read Allan's expression in the dim light cast by the police lanterns as Lestrade's men carefully carried Pauline French up the steps. Phipps leaned wearily against the guard rail, a small defeated figure. Carlotta Adler looked as though she was about to say something, then hurried off to attend to the welfare of the other woman.

"What on earth is going on?" It was Phipps, staring out across the expanse of water to where fleeting moonlight was now picking out the dome of St Paul's. Then, turning to face us, he added bitterly—"I suppose it's occurred to you gentlemen that whoever was responsible for this, it couldn't be any of *us*. We were all at Adler's confounded dinner party."

"Why, he's quite right, Doctor," said Lestrade, turning his questing little face in my direction. "That means either you and Mr Holmes have been on the wrong tack all along . . . or there's more than one party wishes to see this here theatre stays closed."

"Philip Henslowe's ghost, I shouldn't wonder," I replied crossly. I'd just seen the mess my dress trousers were in.

"What did you say?" It was Ted Allan. His body was motionless and his eyes seemed to bore into mine, unless it was a trick of the shifting light. I suddenly realised that I had perhaps said something indiscreet. Holmes had said nothing about not mentioning what we knew about the Rose but I could see now that it might be a trifle tactless to go on with the subject. I was about to mutter some platitude when there came a sound that was all too familiar to a military man like myself.

Somewhere over in the direction of the Globe someone fired a revolver. The sound echoed up and down the silent river.

For a moment everyone stood frozen, as in a tableau. Then Lestrade cried—"Doctor, you come with me. The rest of you stay where you are." He might as well have saved his breath, for as we raced up the jetty steps and across the narrow road that separated it from the Globe, I could hear the sound of footsteps pounding behind us. As we passed the policemen clustered around the cab in which Pauline French was being placed, Lestrade shouted for two of them to follow him. I was vaguely aware of Harry Trent, frozen in the act of paying the other cabbie. Everything seemed to be happening in slow motion.

Ahead of us was the open door through which Adler and Tallis had passed earlier to fetch the wrappings for Miss French. Both of them were standing nearby, frozen to the spot by the sound. Our arrival soon changed that. It was Florenz Adler who took the initiative now.

"Round here to the left," he cried. "It's the quickest way to get to the stage!" We ran into the corridor Holmes and I had taken on our first visit that now seemed an eternity ago.

Then, as we were about half way along it with the auditorium tantalisingly still out of sight, we heard a loud thud as of a heavy dead weight falling and with it a man's scream. "What devilry . . . ?"

I heard myself shouting and then we burst out into the wooden "O".

The moon, which had been playing hide and seek all evening, chose this theatrical moment to break free of a cloud and bathe the surrealistic setting in the kind of spotlight the theatre was never intended to see.

All around us towered the empty galleries, as if tenanted with ghostly spectators. Above the stage was the roof that sheltered the "Heavens" with its painted ceiling now in deepest shadow. Even since our last visit the workmen had been busy with the decoration. The bare wooden stage pillars now had the effect of marble and the painted effigies of classical gods and goddesses stared down on us from every surface. It was as if we had wandered into some strange underworld.

But it was the pool of light on the stage that drew every eye. The noise we had heard was easily explained. A large sack was lying precisely in the middle of it. The fall from the heavens had caused it to split and it was spilling sand from one corner. But what caused me to hold my breath was what lay under the sack. The body of a man, face down where he had clearly fallen under the impact. To his credit, Lestrade was the first to recover his composure. He rushed forward and vaulted on to the stage, no mean feat for a man no longer in his first youth. I was about to follow him when, from the corner of my eye, I saw a hint of movement in the gallery immediately above the stage.

It was the work of a moment to draw my service revolver and take aim. "Stay right where you are," I shouted, "or I shall fire!" Again that slight movement. I let off two shots but heard no sign that I had found the target. I was about to fire again when Lestrade called out in a tone that brooked no argument—"Doctor, I think you'd better come up here. The rest of you, please do as I ask and stay where you are." By now I could see that we had been joined by Carlotta, Allan, Phipps and Trent. The whole of our dinner party, in fact. They were talking among themselves in the kind of hushed whispers usually reserved for church.

With a little help from the Adlers, I scrambled up on the stage and went over to join Lestrade, who was bending over what was clearly a body. "Who is the poor devil?" I asked. "Is it anyone we know?" In a tone I had never heard him use before, Lestrade said quietly—"Yes, Doctor, I'm afraid it is." He gently turned the head of the corpse, so that I could see the face.

I found myself looking at the unmistakable profile of my friend, Sherlock Holmes . . .

Never in my whole life had I known such emptiness. At that moment I literally felt nothing. I was outside myself watching someone else go through this experience. They say a drowning man relives his life in those last few moments and something of the same sort happened to me on that bare stage. I saw Holmes sitting in his favourite chair plucking at that damned fiddle of his . . . I saw the light in his eye which told that the game was afoot once more . . . the tortured indrawn look when he fought his inner demons . . . I saw the two of us putting on our coats to start out on one more journey into doubt and danger . . .

I thought I had plumbed the depths of despair with the episode of the Reichenbach Falls, when Holmes and his arch enemy, Professor Moriarty, had plunged apparently to oblivion and my friend had been lost to the world for three interminable years. At least then I had not been present to witness the event, though my imagination had filled in the details graphically on more than half a hundred occasions.

But now . . . I was possessed with the thought that, while Holmes was in deadly danger, I had been a few short yards away chatting with Lestrade. A few moments, a few paces and I could perhaps have saved him. Now here I was, too late to be of use on this of all occasions. I had even failed to stop the assassin escaping. All of these were the thoughts of this drowning man.

I saw that Lestrade was using his ulster to cover the body. Out of regard for my grief, he covered the waxen face first. "Ingleby . . . Croker . . ." he called out to two of his men, who responded with alacrity, "take good care of—of Mr 'Olmes.

Or you'll have me to deal with. Hop to it, now." The two constables bent over my dear friend like two professional pall bearers and bore the body slowly off the stage into the darkness. I was sure this was not the first time they had been required to perform such a duty.

I found myself rooted to the spot. What had Holmes been doing here instead of joining me at the Adlers' dinner? Why hadn't he confided in me? At least if I'd known the face of our enemy I could and would have pursued him to Doomsday. I felt Lestrade's hand on my arm. "Come along, Doctor, nothing to be gained by staying here. We'll get the devil who did this, don't you worry. Best thing for you is to go home and lie down. Tomorrow morning we'll have all the resources of Scotland Yard on to this."

I let him lead me to the edge of the stage, where helping hands reached out to assist me down. I walked numbly through what was by now a small crowd—Florenz and Carlotta Adler, who pressed my hand in lieu of words. Tallis (as I still thought of him) . . . Allan, Trent and Phipps biting nails that had long since vanished . . . the rest of Lestrade's men. I was conscious of an inarticulate hum of sympathy as Lestrade and I walked past them.

So this was how it all ended—a real life tragedy in the replica of a three hundred year old theatre that had seen some of the greatest fictional tragedies ever staged. Except that this one had an audience of less than a dozen to witness its moonlit drama. Another line from Shakespeare drifted to the surface of my mind—don't ask me why. "Ill met by moonlight." How damnably apt this fellow could be!

The cab ride to Baker Street passed in a blur. I was vaguely aware of Lestrade's helping hand and Mrs Hudson's anxious face as I crossed the threshold of the front door. I remember thinking— "How can she have heard so soon?"—but being guiltily glad that I would not have to be the one to break the dreadful news.

Then I was walking into the familiar sitting room—to be confronted by the massive figure of Mycroft, his hands clasped behind his back.| He spoke, more to Lestrade than to me. "I am grateful you sent your man ahead to find me, Inspector. Your courtesy is much appreciated."

Then to me—"Doctor, we have been here before, you and I. I think deep down both of us knew this day would come. You'll forgive me but I have no words to offer you. My brother asked me to give you this . . ." And he handed me an envelope addressed to me in that well known scrawl.

Somehow, I managed to open my friend's final missive.

My Dear Old Friend,
I hope you never need to read these words,

since that will mean my plans have failed. But as your compatriot, Robbie Burns, has observed, "the best laid plans of mice and men . . ." Somehow I find it reassuring to remember that there have been poets other than Mr W S! I know that you have had occasion to call me insensitive from time to time in relation to people's feelings but I am deeply sensitive of how you will now be feeling. The Reichenbach business proved that in no uncertain terms and I have no intention of having you relive those days. In the past I have often asked you to attempt the impossible and I do it one last time. I cannot bear to think that Holmes and Watson failed Queen and Country when the great call came and I know I can count on you to act for us both. Lestrade has his instructions. Work with him, as you would with me, and all will still be well.

Let me tell you here what I could never find the words for in your presence. Without Watson, there would *be* no Holmes.

Your friend—SHERLOCK HOLMES

I felt myself clutching the paper as the room spun round and a black mist enclosed me.

CHAPTER THIRTEEN

I presume Mycroft and Lestrade somehow got me to bed and I have a vague recollection of someone—presumably a police doctor—bending over me and administering a sedative. After that I fell back into the abyss.

I found myself dreaming the strangest things. I was standing on the stage of the Globe totally alone. All around me the galleries of the wooden "O" were packed with all the people I had ever known in my life. Although none of them appeared to be speaking, I could hear the sounds of their voices inside my head.

There were men I'd served with at the battle of Maiwand, many of whom I'd seen fall in action. There was my first wife, Mary, looking as young and lovely as the day I met her. There were faces from the various cases Holmes and I had investigated—Irene Adler, the glowering Grimsby Rylott from "The Speckled Band," the carrot topped Jabez Wilson of "The Red-Headed League." Some appeared more than once. I could see several Mycrofts and Lestrades. Dotted among these familiar faces were the characters from this latest drama . . . a much younger Dame Ivy, whispering into the ear of Simon Phipps, who appears more concerned to arrange his green carnation just so . . . Allan and Trent staring at each other impassively from opposite galleries . . . the three Adlers sitting together like a model family . . . Pauline French dressed as Ophelia and appearing not to notice the water streaming from her clothes. And everywhere I look there is Holmes. Holmes in all the moods I know so well . . . pensive, brooding, ironic . . . and always staring right into my eyes and saying—"Don't worry, old friend, all will be well. All manner of things will be well."

Now I realise they are all waiting for me to do something but I am tongue tied. Then I hear the voice of Mrs Hudson saying—"I hate to disturb you, Doctor, but there's a gentleman come to pay his respects. It's Mr Adler. What am I to say?" I struggled through the mists of sleep back to reality.

As my eyes began to focus, I saw that Mrs Hudson was dressed entirely in black and the events of the previous evening came flooding back. As if reading my mind, she held out a copy of the morning paper. One of the leading stories was headlined—"SHERLOCK HOLMES DEAD! DETECTIVE KILLED IN TRAGIC ACCIDENT." The rest of the story had obviously been provided to the reporter by Lestrade and told how, in the hurry to finish the theatre for this evening's gala opening, workmen had failed to adequately secure certain building materials, which had then fallen on to the temporary stage just as the famous detective was crossing it. What he was doing there was not made clear. This appalling accident, etc., etc.

Mrs Hudson interrupted my reading. "There's Mr Adler to see you, Doctor, if you're feeling up to it. Mr Mycroft had a word with me last night before he left. He said we must all carry on as normal. It's as Mr Holmes would have wanted it. But it'll be dreadful hard, Doctor—dreadful hard." She seemed about to say something else but her emotions overcame her and putting her apron up to her eyes, she fled the room.

My heart went out to the poor soul. For all her scolding, I knew her to be devoted to Holmes. In many ways we were both the sons to her that she had never had and now one of them was gone—once more. For myself my overriding sensation was one of numbness—the lingering effects of the sedative, I assumed. Slowly and methodically I concentrated on dressing to face the bleakness of the day ahead.

A few minutes later I was shaking Florenz Adler's hand. Just as the impresario had shown himself capable of appearing larger than his real size, now he seemed to have shrunk. The fight had gone out of him. "Doctor, I owe you an apology. Holmes, too, if only he were here to hear it. If I hadn't been so pigheaded about building this crazy theatre . . ."

"Come, Adler," I said, summoning up as much conviction as I could, when all I really wanted to do was sit and feel sorry for myself, "you mustn't blame yourself for the actions of a maniac. You may have found yourself the lightning conductor but you're certainly not the lightning."

"At least lightning strikes cleanly," said Adler bitterly. "Allan skulks around in the dark." Then seeing the dawning surprise on my face, he quickly added—"Yes, Mr Holmes has taken me into his confidence—posthumously." And he tapped a bulky document I now noticed in his jacket pocket. "When I got back to the hotel after . . ." he didn't need to complete the sentence—"I received a visit from Mr Holmes's elder brother . . ." Mycroft, I reflected, had indeed been busy. "He said he had been given a note to deliver to me in the event of anything happening to Mr Holmes. In it he gave me the outline of what he knows—*knew*—and asked me to be sure the show went on as planned. He said it was the only way we had any chance to contain Allan and possibly unmask him . . . force him into doing something to give us the evidence we need to bring him to justice.

"It goes without saying, Doctor, that I shall do as he asks, if only out of respect for his memory. And, Doctor, don't think me heartless if I haven't said the right thing about him but for once I'm plumb out of the right thing to say. Forgive me."

There was a moment of silence and in that moment I felt closer to the man than I had so far.

It was the impresario who spoke first. "After last night I was beginning to wonder if I had the right to continue but Holmes's note has taken that decision out of my hands. Even so, a couple of things keep nagging at the back of my mind. In his letter Holmes insists that, whatever other cast changes I may be forced to make, Carlotta must appear as Gertrude. Now, frankly, she was devas-tated by what happened and I'd intended to keep her out of harm's way but, as soon as I told her what Holmes had said, she point blank refused to have any of it. She insists on appearing, so that's that."

"You said two things bothered you?"

"Yes. How in blazes did Allan manage to kill Holmes? Surely he was with one or more of us all evening?"

Immediately my mind replayed the snapshots of those frenzied moments. Where *had* we seen Allan and when? He'd arrived at the Globe after the Adlers and myself but surely he'd been in the cab with Carlotta and Phipps? Could he have left them long enough to set up the device that trapped my friend? But then he had interrupted my conversation with Lestrade. And I recalled his quoting the Ophelia speech. After I heard the shot my impression of things went by in a blur. Who had fired a revolver? Not Holmes, for he wasn't carrying one to the best of my knowledge. The man in the gallery that I shot at? Did he sever the rope with a bullet? I made a mental note to ask Lestrade. And had Allan had time in the confusion to reach the gallery by another entrance before we entered the wooden "O"?

My dulled brain couldn't cope with all the complexities involved. In any case, what did it matter? My friend was dead and all that now mattered was that Allan be brought to book.

A few minutes later Adler left. As I went to shake his hand, he took mine in both of his. "Until this afternoon, Doctor. As Holmes said—we all have our parts to play and, God willing . . ." I was still standing there when the door below banged shut.

I went to the sideboard and, regardless of the time of day, poured myself a large whisky and soda, which I took over to my chair. It seemed strange to be sitting opposite Holmes's empty chair, knowing he would never occupy it again. When this business was over, I should have the macabre duty of shutting up these rooms, the scene of so many triumphs and tragedies. How could one pack up so much history, so many memories? But that was tomorrow's task. Today we must play out the game to whatever conclusion was intended. After which, I should make it my business to hound Edward Allan to the ends of the earth, if need be.

I determined to think things through as Holmes would have done. What did we know and what might we infer? We knew the identity of the killer and we had good reason to believe—with this added conviction of Freud's professional analysis—that his frenzy was building to some kind of crescendo, exacerbated by Adler's stubborn refusal to abandon his Globe project. Allan's madness—I had to keep thinking of him as Allan or lose my own grip on events—had now transcended the idea of the Globe versus the Rose and become morbidly attached to the people involved.

Carlotta was now effectively Gertrude and must be punished in some way for betraying his unknown natural father with Adler, now irrevocably cast as Claudius. So that the plot must be played out. Was *Hamlet* the key to everything? And what about the death of Holmes? Had the Dame Ivy episode triggered thoughts of Polonius, as Holmes had suggested? And had Holmes himself become the next "wretched, rash, intruding fool" in Allan's demented drama? Where did the real Queen fit in? Was she to pay for an earlier queen's failure to prefer the Rose to the upstart Globe?

It was then that I realised that we were soon to have many of those answers provided for us without further effort on our part. There was a sinking feeling in my stomach as I remembered part of the previous evening's dinner conversation. Asked if he had decided on the running order for the gala performance, Adler had replied that he intended to "open the show with a bang" by staging the duel scene—from *Hamlet*! If I was to serve Holmes's memory it would have to be through some form of action not theory. In a strange way the thought gave me comfort.

I decided that to preserve my sanity I needed to get out of the house for a while and pass among ordinary people who behaved in a simple, straightforward way, saying what they believed and living by decent, simple values.

As I finished dressing, I noticed a plain black band that Mrs Hudson had tactfully provided. Slipping it on my arm almost caused me to lose my carefully contrived composure. Holmes's "death" at Reichenbach had been a clean, cold shock but this was somehow worse.

I am nothing if not a creature of habit and it occurred to me that the routine of lunching at my club might well provide the necessary discipline to get me through this day. In that I was soon proved wrong. The food was like sawdust in my mouth and the condolences of my fellow members, whether expressed or implied, soon became more than I could bear. Leaving the table with as much dignity as I could muster, I decided to take a walk through St James's Park.

Whatever the rest of the day might hold, the Globe would have magnificent weather for its rebirth. The sun was warm on the skin and seemed to have brought everyone out of doors. There were couples walking arm in arm, the ladies still bright in their summer dresses. Nannies perambulated their charges, the more adventurous allowing them to feed the ducks. Dotted among the crowd were occasional military uniforms. The news from South Africa was worsening by the day and I knew enough to recognise their insignia and tell that these were men most likely enjoying their last days before their ship sailed. It brought back memories of my own service days and suddenly some of the warmth seemed to go out of the sun.

I decided to sit on one of the benches and look out over the lake for a few minutes. I must have been off in a world of my own, when I heard a voice say—"Doctor Watson, may I interrupt you for a few moments?"

I looked up to find Simon Phipps standing in front of me and with him, slightly holding back, Pauline French. They both looked tired and nervous and I had the distinct impression from her body language that the girl had been encouraging him to make the approach. It was hard to say which of us was the more awkward, as I rose and raised my hat to Miss French.

"Most certainly," I replied, indicating that they should join me on the seat. Now that he had plucked up his courage to speak, there was no stopping Phipps. The strain of the previous evening was entirely gone. Here was a man who had decided to tackle his personal demons and take his chances. For the first time I saw something behind the facade he'd been constructing and I fancy I know enough about women to venture a guess that Miss French had something to do with the change in him.

"Doctor Watson," he burst out, "I behaved like an absolute fool last night. I thought that I had the cares of the world on my shoulders and it was only when that terrible business with Mr Holmes and nearly losing Pauline . . ." As I tried to summon up the appropriate expression, I couldn't help but notice her place her hand reassuringly on his arm. My instincts on that first meeting at the Globe had been correct after all.

"I've been awake all night thinking things over and then, when they let Pauline come home this morning, I went round and told her everything . . ."

"And I said he should talk to you," that lady added.

In the next half hour it all came pouring out. His experiences in the United States, the saloon brawl and the accidental death that resulted. How he arrived in England and was accepted by Adler for the new Globe company and a corner seemed to have been turned. He described how he and

Pauline had met and become attracted to one another. At which point Miss French smiled and I could well see why.

"But then it all started to unravel, Doctor." The strained look started to creep back into his face. "Ted Allan—or whatever his infernal name is—joined the company and he was soon in cahoots with Dame Ivy. They clearly found they had some interest in common—don't ask me what. Then one day Allan takes me aside and makes it clear that he knows all about San Francisco and maybe Flo Adler and the local police here might like to know, too. Oh, don't worry, Doctor," he interpreted my questioning glance, "I've told Pauline everything.

"Well, the last thing I want to do is to open that can of worms over again. I could lose everything I've got"—and he looked at Pauline—"or hope to have. To cut a long story short, I was weak. He said he might need help with his Grand Plan—I swear that was the phrase he used. His Grand Plan. He never told me what it was. He saw me as just a spear carrier, I suppose. Dame Ivy was clearly Lady Macbeth or something equally imposing. He said he'd let me know when it was my turn to enter. He talked like that.

"Doctor, he is really strange. One moment he can be quite normal and a perfectly charming, intelligent man. Then, in the middle of a sentence a look will come into his eye and he's suddenly someone quite different. I tell you this, he scares me a whole lot more than that man in the San Francisco bar! I tried to put it all to the back of my mind—and then this Fiske business came up.

"One evening I was handed a message scribbled on a piece of paper—I think I still have it somewhere. It was from Allan telling me to come to some public house right away and some quotation—he was always quoting Shakespeare—about 'It is the cause, my soul.' Something like that. *Othello*, I think, but it doesn't matter. I arrived to find he'd got Fiske completely drunk. He pretended it was all a big joke. Ham wanted to find a new way to play Richard the Third and we were going to help him. Anyway, we got him into that square and propped him up on the statue. Then I left them to it. I couldn't get out of there fast enough.

"Well, as you know, it turned out that there was more to it than that. And if the police say I was an accessory . . . Oh, don't worry, Doctor, as soon as today's over, I'm going to see them . . . well, I expect I'll have a hard time proving otherwise.

"And then, of course, there was Oxford. That was Allan again, wanting to know what you and Mr Holmes were up to. 'They come not single spies, but in battalions,' he said, which I thought a strange way of putting it. I fancied myself quite a good actor but Mr Holmes spotted me in a moment. I only wish he were here so that I could apologise to him, too.

221

"And there you have it, Doctor. Please don't say anything. I know what I have to do. I just wanted you to know and when we called at Baker Street, your housekeeper was kind enough to let us know where we might find you. I think she realised our business was pretty urgent. So we waited outside your club and—here we are. Thank you for listening so patiently."

He seemed to have finished unburdening himself but before I could say anything by way of response, he blurted out—"Look, I know this is the last thing you need right now but you know so much about these things after all your years with . . ." He didn't complete the sentence. "Aren't the police going to do something to stop this maniac? I know a man's guilty until he's proved innocent but I'd swear he did something to Ham Fiske, he *must* have killed poor old Ivy and then last night . . . I've wracked my brains all night but I still can't work out how he did it . . . those men he must have hired to drown Pauline and then Mr Holmes . . ."

His voice trailed away and I heard myself saying with a lot more confidence than I felt—"Don't worry, Mr Phipps. Allan will not evade the long arm of justice. The police and I have planned for every eventuality. Even now the net is tightening." At my back I could almost hear Holmes whispering—"Watson, you really must avoid using so many cliches in your little narratives." The thought almost caused me to miss what Pauline French was saying.

"Simon, be a dear and let me have two minutes with Doctor Watson, will you?" With a boyish gesture Phipps reached out his hand and shook mine, rather as a schoolboy would take his leave from his headmaster at the end of term. A few moments later he had taken up a position a few yards away, leaning on a railing and watching the ducks for which the park is justly famous.

"Doctor, I'm well aware that everything is going to come out in the next few hours, so I'm probably worrying you unnecessarily but could you please put my mind at rest on one thing? I haven't said anything about this to anyone, not even Simon, because I promised I wouldn't, but since you obviously know about it anyway . . . why did Mr Holmes and Inspector Lestrade arrange for me to pretend to be drowning last night?"

I didn't believe anything more could happen to surprise me in my present state but I was woefully wrong. In a flash I realised that—in my grief over the death of Holmes—I hadn't given a though to "Ophelia's" drowning. Of course. How could Allan have arranged it, unless—as Phipps suggested—he had hired someone to do it for him? And yet I would have sworn that it was Allan's style to act alone and almost certainly motivated by impulse. So Holmes and Lestrade had contrived the incident, presumably to shock Allan into thinking he was not alone in opposing the Globe and perhaps destabilise his dementia until they had gained enough time to get past the royal opening and gather enough evidence to arrest him? So Pauline French had been Holmes's mystery luncheon guest? A pattern was beginning to emerge, though some of the biggest pieces were tantalisingly out of reach. Was the death of Holmes Allan's frenzied reaction to the Ophelia incident? Did he detect Holmes's hand in it? But no, that piece didn't fit either. . . .

I was conscious that Pauline was still waiting for my answer. Summoning up my most avuncular manner, I patted the small hand that rested on my arm. "Don't you worry, my dear. Sherlock Holmes never did anything without a purpose. All will be revealed. If you play your part on that stage today half as well as you did last night, I know Holmes would have been proud of you. No, go and look after that young man of yours . . ." With a smile that reminded me of another young lady departed these many years, she ran over to where Phipps was standing. The last I saw of them they were walking down the path away from me. I saw her slip her arm though his and, although I may have been imagining it, I thought their step seemed lighter.

CHAPTER FOURTEEN

I had the cab drop me at the approach to Southwark Bridge Road. The weather continued fine and I felt that it would calm me to walk the rest of the way and organise my thoughts. On an impulse I didn't fully understand myself, I had slipped my service revolver into my pocket, as Holmes so often bade me do. Precisely what good it would do me in a crowd I had no idea but its presence gave me a little much-needed comfort.

As I descended the steps that took me down to the river walkway, I became part of a steady stream of people all heading in the same direction. On the road above us hansom after hansom was decanting its cargo of passengers to swell the throng.

They were a good tempered crowd, chattering loudly in anticipation of being about to witness a unique event—Shakespeare's return to Bankside and the rebirth of the "great Globe itself". Now we could see it rising some thirty feet and towering over the surrounding buildings, just as it must have done some three hundred years ago. Now its white sides gleamed in the afternoon sun but a London winter would soon take care of that and it would blend into the background just as though it had never been away. I couldn't help notice how people's voices suddenly dropped when they first caught sight of it, for it was indeed a magnificent sight. I could well see why men had pursued the dream of rebuilding it for so long. Ironic to think it had taken a brash American to give us back such an important part of our heritage.

Jostled by the crowds who were now finding their voices as they entered the building, I found myself pushed along the familiar corridor and into the sunlight of the wooden "O". I have to confess I was stunned by what I saw. Gone were the builders and their debris, their sawhorses and dust sheets. There was the stage that had already seen its share of drama, now covered with rushes. There were the mighty stage pillars that one would have taken for marble, if you didn't know that they were painted wood. And there, above and around the stage itself the carved and brightly painted effigies of mythical gods and goddesses. Within those few short days—while so much that was black and evil had been taking place in the real world—a universe of dreams had been taking shape. And now here it was, magnificent and complete and nothing must be allowed to dim its luster.

I must have been lost in my own thoughts for I was quite startled to feel a hand on my sleeve. I looked round to find a small figure in a well worn tweed suit and sporting a flat cap of the kind most often seen on the grouse moor. And even allowing that we were now well past the "glorious twelfth", it looked a little out of place in an Elizabethan playhouse. As if he could read my mind, the man quickly removed it and stuffed it into his pocket, brushing unruly hair flat with his hand like a small schoolboy. It was then that I realised who my companion was.

"Good afternoon, Doctor Watson," said Professor Campbell Bryson, "you seem surprised to see me." Indeed I was but a moment's thought sufficed to resolve that. Elizabethan playhouses were, after all, his special subject and his next remark completed the picture. "Your visit the other day with Mr Holmes piqued my curiosity and I thought—'I must see what sort of a mess that Adler feller's made of things'." Then a realisation struck him. "Oh, my dear Doctor, what must you think of me? I only heard the appalling news as I got off the train and bought a paper. My heartiest condolences. The world has lost a great intellect."

"Yes," I replied gruffly, "and I a great friend." I looked away over his shoulder at the crowded galleries while I fought to keep my emotions under control. Then I returned my attention to the crestfallen academic. "So what sort of mess *has* he made, Professor?"

That was enough to distract him back to safer ground. "Very creditable, very creditable, I must admit. Personally, I still believe the stage pillars are wrongly placed and one could argue whether Thalia and Melpomene"—and here he indicated the elaborately carved figures of two buxom goddesses—"should be stage left or stage right but otherwise . . . very creditable indeed. Seeing it in all its glory—for it does take one back across the centuries, does it not?—one can quite see how the poor little Rose was outclassed. And now, what play shall we hear today, I wonder?"

I was in the midst of telling him what little I knew of the day's events when I observed the figure of Lestrade pushing through the crowd in my direction. "Ah, Doctor, looking for you everywhere," he said, removing the bowler hat he affected whatever the weather and mopping his brow. As he did so, he looked questioningly at the Professor.

"Lestrade, I don't believe you've met . . ." I said and made the introductions.

"Delighted to meet you, Professor," said the Inspector, "you're just the chap the Doctor and I need to explain to us what's going on. It'll be double Dutch to us, I shouldn't wonder . . ."

"Speak for yourself, Lestrade," I replied somewhat irritably, "I've been a Shakespeare man all my life." With that, Lestrade dropped the subject and steered us towards the back of the crowd until we were standing as close as we could get to the roped off section of the lower gallery which would hold the royal party.

As we pushed and jostled, I muttered into Lestrade's ear—"There are a few things you and I need to discuss, Lestrade. I've been talking to Miss French about last night . . ." If the back of a man's head can blush, Lestrade's did just that.

Out of the side of his mouth I heard him say— "All in good time, Doctor. As soon as this lot is over, I promise!" And with that I had to be content.

Bryson seemed surprised that we did not move up into the gallery itself, until Lestrade, glancing pointedly at me, said: "The Doctor and I are men of the people, eh, Doctor? We know our place." Then, so that the professor couldn't hear—"My men are mingling with the crowd, just in case, and I promised 'your friend' that we'd stay as near as possible." I nodded to show I understood.

It's unlikely that we needed to take any such care in conversing, for Bryson was in a world that was more real to him than the one the rest of us inhabited.

"Quite right, quite right—we shall be Groundlings. They were the people who stood here in the yard. Fifteen hundred of them when the place was full and another fifteen hundred packing the galleries . . ."

I looked up to where the rows of backless benches were rapidly filling with a cross section of society. On our level were the better and more formally dressed, most of them there by royal invitation. Above us and in the "wings" curling around the stage the clothes were brighter and the accents broader, while the yard itself was peopled by as cheerful a crowd of Londoners as you would expect to see on Hampstead Heath on a bank holiday, which for them it virtually was.

Bryson's voice broke in again. "All London came here to 'hear a play' and meet their friends. Clerks, courtesans and cutpurses. Ladies of repute and those of less certain reputation, lords, merchants and miscreants. It was a true melting pot of Elizabethan society and the plays were their newspapers, for many of those three thousand were illiterate, you know. They came here both for discourse and distraction and somehow the theatre itself made them all one. Can't you feel it beginning to happen even now, gentlemen?"

And strangely, I began to sense what he meant. Unlike any theatre I could recall, there was a unity among that very diverse audience. It was something to do with the intimacy created by that encircling shape that enabled each one of you to be aware of everyone else. We were all part of a greater entity and part of the play, even before it began.

"They used to call the audience 'The Great Beast', you know and it was up to the actors to tame it with their performance." Bryson continued. "I wonder if the beast will turn and rend today?" His words sent a shiver along my spine and suddenly I remembered just why I was standing here and wondered what might happen beneath that warm September sky.

Realising that the professor was three hundred years away, I turned aside to Lestrade. "Is everything under control?"

"Everything we can possibly think of, Doctor," he replied. "Of course, we're pretty sure he's acting alone but just in case he has any accomplices . . . My men are all over the theatre and I've a couple who'll be in that dressing room place"—he indicated the back of the stage—"the moment they're all out there. Oh, there is *one* rummy thing . . ."

My heart sank. "For God's sake, man—what's that?"

"Adler's vanished. Not a smell of him anywhere. Seems to have gone off without a word to anyone."

"But isn't he in the first scene? I thought he was playing the King in the duel scene?"

"So he was, Doctor, so he was. He was also supposed to greet Her Majesty when she arrives but we got a message earlier today that the lady wants her party to arrive without fuss and meet everybody *after* the performance. Let's hope he turns up by then. Luckily, young Tallis has stepped into the breach on the acting front. Seems he's played the part in an amateur production. He's going to carry a script, just in case, but he seems pretty sure he can fill in for his father. Rather him than me."

I found my mind racing with possibilities. Was this part of Holmes's plan and, if so, how did it fit? Or had Allan decided on a desperate throw at the last moment by eliminating the man he saw as the arch villain in his own Grand-Guignol? And, most important, what would Holmes expect of me in these new circumstances?

Before I could arrange my thoughts into any semblance of order, I was aware of a ripple of movement near the entrance to the theatre that was closest to the river. A trumpeter blew a fanfare from the stage gallery. The general babble of noise died down to a murmur as all heads turned to see what had caused it. Then the crowd near the entrance parted like the waters of the Red Sea and a loud if ragged cheer went up. All around us the people in the galleries began to rise to their feet and join in the cheering as the royal party could be seen entering.

Next to me Bryson whispered loudly—"Not *the* Queen but at least a Queen. Better late than never, eh?"

And now the party were approaching where we stood. There were several solidly built members of the Brigade of Guards, I was pleased to see, flanking Her Majesty's personal retinue. Next came the elegant patrician figure of the Marquess of Salisbury, the Prime Minister, and on the other side, dwarfing him, the bulk of Mycroft Holmes. As he passed, his eye caught mine and the merest flicker of expression disturbed his impassivity.

Then I concentrated on the woman who had ruled much of the civilised world since before I and most of the people around me had been born. I had seen her many times over the years on occasions such as this and the sight never ceased to make me feel proud.

Today I also felt a little sad. She was being carried in a sort of semi-covered sedan borne by four sturdy fellows in livery and I remembered reading that her doctors had confined her to bed for the past several days. She was, of course, an old lady now, though her spirit made that hard to accept. I had no doubt that today, in her determination to be here, the royal will had triumphed over the medical. I could see that her face was mostly covered from air that would turn chilly later by some sort of lacy—"mantilla" was the word that came to mind, though my wife would undoubtedly tell me it was something quite other. Her gloved hands were clasped around a silver topped cane. My overriding thought was that nothing should happen to this gallant lady, if John H. Watson had any say in the matter.

As the crowd settled, I turned to Lestrade. "Well, Lestrade, I suppose all you have to worry about now is getting her safely out of here? The worst is over." Lestrade didn't appear to share my *sangfroid*.

He seemed about to say something when there

were three sharp knocks on the floor of the stage—the classic sign that the entertainment was about to begin.

Two actors entered. Allan dressed in the funereal garb of Hamlet, Prince of Denmark, returned to court from his exile and now accompanied by his old friend, Horatio, played by Harrison Trent. As they stroll about chatting, they are approached by a Lord bidding Hamlet attend the King and Queen's pleasure. There is to be a fencing bout between Hamlet and Laertes, brother of the dead Ophelia. Having delivered his message, the Lord exits.

HORATIO: You will lose, my lord.
HAMLET: I do not think so . . .

Then I fancied I saw something in Allan's face which went unnoticed by almost everyone else in that audience. He seemed to withdraw, leaving the face a mask. Others would perceive it as an actor internalising his thoughts but I found myself wondering precisely who I was watching at that moment. Allan? Lowe? Hamlet? Or some hybrid creature compounded of all of them? On stage Hamlet was telling Horatio that he would "win at the odds". He went on . . .

HAMLET: . . . thou wouldst not think how ill all's here about my heart. But it is no matter.

234

With a sudden sickening feeling I realised that the lines themselves were beginning to affect the man, tip him further away from reality and over the edge into some other world where he could no longer be reached by reason.

HAMLET: There is a special providence in the fall of a sparrow. If it be now, 'tis not to come; if it be not to come, it will be now; if it be not now, yet it will come. The readiness is all . . .

The light the words kindled in Allan's eyes was unearthly. Freud was right. We were not dealing with one man but several. And out of the abyss was clambering—who? Holmes had lost his gamble but what could I do? I could hardly climb up on that stage and say—what? I fingered my trusty service revolver and tried to concentrate on what was happening in the play.

The stage was now filled with the other actors who made up the duel scene. King Claudius— a surprisingly authoritative Tallis, discreetly carrying a text. Carlotta Adler as his Queen Gertrude looking distinctly nervous, I thought— as well she might. Sundry lords and courtiers carrying cushions, chairs and flagons of wine. As they settled themselves, Simon Phipps made his way through the crowd in his role as Laertes. Once again, I realised I may have been reading what I already knew into people's expressions but I would have said that here was a man who was once again his own man, for good or ill. All he now wanted was this game over and done with.

On the stage the King is bringing the two contestants together to reconcile them before the contest. Even while Allan was speaking the lines to Laertes, his gaze was fixed on Tallis and he might as well have substituted the words he was clearly thinking—"What are *you* doing here? Where is the man I have pursued for so long— where is *Adler?*" As it was, he was saying . . .

> What I have done . . . I here proclaim was
> madness . . . His madness is poor Hamlet's
> enemy . . .

For some reason this seemed to disconcert Phipps and I saw Tallis sneak a surreptitious glance at his script. Then at my elbow Bryson whispered something which worried me even more: "He's cutting his lines. Why is he cutting the lines?"

At that moment I knew with a dread certainty that we were watching a play within a play. Inside his spinning brain, Allan was snatching at the words of his character and holding on to those that made sense of his own turmoil. When the words no longer fitted or—worse still—when they were exchanged for violent action on that stage, what then?

The swords were being selected . . .

> LAERTES: This is too heavy. Let me see another.
> HAMLET: This likes me well. These swords have all a length?

An attendant assured him they did.

> KING: Set me the stoups of wine upon that table—
> If Hamlet give the first or second hit
> Or quit in answer of the first exchange,
> Let all the battlements their ordnance fire . . .

And now the duel began. Both men were light on their feet but Allan clearly had the advantage and, while Phipps was clearly going through a series of motions as they had been rehearsed, I could see his expression begin to tighten around the mouth. Something was happening that had *not* been rehearsed. Allan was really attacking him. Had it not been for the buttons on the foils, the situation might have become dangerous. Laertes' "Come, my lord" had hardly been necessary.

Then, as in the play, Hamlet made the first contact.

HAMLET: One
LAERTES: No
HAMLET: Judgement!
COURTIER: A hit, a very palpable hit.
LAERTES: Well, again

At this the King snatched a goblet of wine to toast Hamlet's success. At my elbow I realised that Bryson had been conducting a non-stop commentary on the stage action, as much to himself as to Lestrade and me.

"See, the king puts a poisoned pearl into the wine to kill off Hamlet but, of course, Hamlet doesn't drink it . . ."

KING: Give him the cup.
HAMLET: I'll play this bout first. Set it by awhile.

Something now seemed to be troubling Bryson. His voice rose to a bleat, so that heads near us turned in irritation. He moderated his tone to a hoarse whisper into my ear. "*Hamlet's* not supposed to set the cup aside. And why is *he* putting something into it. The King's already done that . . ."

And, indeed, masked by the other activity of the court scene—with people moving and talking on the stage, while waiting for the fencing to resume, Allan had indeed taken the cup Tallis offered and moved around the stage pillar, while practising feinting movements with his rapier. Tallis and Phipps exchanged puzzled looks but they had clearly ceased to be surprised by anything Allan did. In any event, his back was now turned to them briefly and prevented them from seeing what he did next, which was to take folded piece of paper from inside his robe and tip its contents into the wine. Then, completing his move around the pillar, he replaced the goblet on the table next to the Queen and pointed his sword at Laertes.

HAMLET: Come.

A few more movements and then . . .

HAMLET: Another hit. What say you?
LAERTES: A touch, a touch, I do confess it.

On stage the courtiers are showing their excitement at Hamlet's success but at least two of the Groundlings have somewhat different feelings. Bryson continues to complain: "Absolutely nothing in either the Quarto or Folio versions to justify such a vulgar interpolation. If *this* is the sort of thing Adler's going to . . . ." For my part, my mind was racing in an attempt to try and understand what I had just seen. Was this a piece of stage business or something far more sinister? I looked at Lestrade. Had he noticed it, too? He seemed more concerned to scan the crowd, presumably to spot the whereabouts of his own men. Before I could say anything to him, the action began again.

Carlotta was picking up the goblet and raising it to her son.

QUEEN: The Queen carouses to thy fortune, Hamlet.
HAMLET: Good madam
KING: Gertrude, do not drink
QUEEN: I will, my lord. I pray you, pardon me.

She then drank and replaced the cup. There was a pause that seemed to hush the theatre, as mother and son looked at each other for a long moment. Allan was facing in my direction and, once again, I saw that play of emotions cross his lean face. If the good Dr Freud were right, several different people were struggling to find release from within that tortured mind. As the silence stretched on the expression that seemed to prevail was that of a lost and frightened little boy.

"Has the fool forgotten his lines?" Bryson hissed. " 'I dare not drink yet, madam—by and by.' Come along, man!"

In a dull monotone that could hardly be heard

Allan said, as if accepting Bryson's cue—"I dare not drink yet, mother."

"Madam—not 'Mother'—*Madam*." Bryson was almost beside himself. On the stage the actors were looking at one another helplessly. Then Carlotta rose unsteadily to her feet and stretched out a hand to Allan . . . "The drink! Oh, my dear son. The drink!" Then she slid to the floor and lay there motionless.

"My God, Lestrade!" I cried, "we must do something. That devil's poisoned her!" The Inspector looked at me with an expression that positively willed me to listen to him. "Our place is right here. Trust me, Doctor." And to be fair to that honest soul, I had no idea what else I could do.

The audience was buzzing, very much as its Elizabethan equivalent must have done. Some of them presumably knew the play well enough, though I suspect most knew only the broad outlines of the plot. All of them could sense that something out of the ordinary was going on in front of their eyes but was it part of this unique theatrical experience they had been told so much about?

I resolved not to take my eyes off Allan. Whatever transpired, I would be the one witness who could attest to his every move. As the rest of the cast stood rooted to the spot, he knelt next to the Queen.

HAMLET: Oh, villainy! Ho! Let the door
be locked Treachery! Seek it out.

Once again he shielded himself from the other
principals, though not from me. I saw him quickly
remove the protective "button" from the tip of
his foil. The vulnerable child was gone and in its
place someone or something whose eyes were
dead.

Then something happened which I swear
raised the hair on the back of my head and even
silenced Bryson. As the audience were transfixed
by the frozen tableau of actors, the double doors
at the rear of the stage crashed open. There on a
dais and surrounded by mist stood an unearthly
giant of a man.

He stood fully seven feet tall and the wide
brimmed hat he wore made him taller still. He
was dressed in a black mantle that covered him
from head to toe and around his neck was a deep
white ruff lace collar. The chalk white face was
heavily bearded and the eyes seemed to glow. I
was sure the being, whoever he was, could see
into my soul and from the way those around me
were holding their breath, I was not alone in my
reaction.

The utter silence that fell on the theatre may
only have lasted a few seconds. All I know is that
it seemed an eternity. While it lasted I began to
feel a memory stir at the back of my mind. I had

seen this man before—but where? Bryson proved the answer. In a very small voice he said— "Edward Alleyn."

That was it. "The Gentleman from Dulwich" in the portrait Holmes had borrowed. The leading actor in Henslowe's Rose company. Before I could pursue the thought further, "Alleyn" spoke.

Slowly—oh, so slowly—he raised his right arm and pointed unmistakably at Allan and in a voice that seemed to echo and re-echo around the wooden "O" . . .

> Put up your sword, rash youth, tho' your intent
> Was noble at its birth, yet does it stale
> And fall from honour. Now 'tis nothing worth.
> Alleyn and Henslowe. Henslowe and Alleyn -
> Two names that shook the heavens in their day
> That day is gone, yet still we walk with gods,
> Our fame is in the firmament writ large
> And needs no champion here to plead its cause.
> You do but vex our shades. Prithee, begone!
> Our wish is that Will's Globe may live again.

Allan's face was a picture. I've heard of someone's jaw dropping but his literally did. He spun around to look at his fellow actors and found they were as stunned as he was by the apparition. Then he turned back to face it once again. Slowly he dropped to his knees, as if in supplication. But as he did so, his body was shaken by a sudden convulsion. He clapped his free hand to his head and let out a feral scream that chilled the blood of everyone in that auditorium.

As its echoes died away, I realised there was complete silence in the theatre. All attention was on that lonely figure. It was the only thing moving on that vast stage as slowly Allan rose to his feet, turned and faced actors and audience. Then you could hear a collective gasp. Clearly the man had had some form of seizure. One side of his face had lost control and drooped as if made of some soft substance. His right arm also hung loosely by his side. But it was his eyes—my God, his eyes! They were the eyes of the wild creature that lurks deep in the forest of one's worst nightmare.

More pieces of the puzzle fell into place. He was holding the sword in his *left* hand. The left hand emphasis in the typed notes . . . the left handed "stabbing" of Caesar. But we were past the point where such clues could serve any useful purpose. The man was still lethal.

And then he moved. Despite his affliction, he lurched forward with remarkable speed towards the front of the stage. At which point I realised—

two Queens! He'd killed one and now he meant to have the other. Lestrade had obviously come to precisely the same conclusion. "Come on, Doctor. It's our turn now." And he began to force his way through the crowd. As I followed through the path he cleared, I took out my service revolver but, even as I did so, I asked myself how I could possibly use it without risking innocent lives.

In situations such as this, people invariably behave like sheep, moving the wrong way even when they're trying to help. Quick as we were, Allan was quicker. Just as he reached the edge of the stage, Phipps realised something of his intention and threw himself in front of the man. Without stopping, Allan slashed at him with his foil. Had it been a true sword, who knows what might have happened. As it was, the uncapped point cut through Phipps's forearm and I saw the shirt sleeve redden dramatically.

The next moment Allan's misshapen figure was on the ground and limping across the yard, slashing with his foil at anyone near him. The crowd melted before him, as if fearful of contagion. Lestrade and I were still several feet from the royal party and I could see the equerries moving towards the VIPs in what seemed like slow motion, though I suppose that was merely how it seemed to my shocked mind. Frozen as in a photograph, I saw a lady-in-waiting, her hand to her mouth to suppress a scream. I saw Mycroft, his hand poised over the Queen's shoulder. But the image that burned into my brain was of the Queen herself. In the midst of the noise and panic she sat perfectly still in her seat, her gaze fixed unwaveringly on the approaching Allan.

They say a wild dog can be deterred from attacking, if one stares it down and the irrelevant thought crossed my mind that this was precisely what she was trying to do. Certainly it had the effect of stopping him some ten feet from the gallery rail that separated them.

Why did no one move? It was as though the whole crowd were under a spell and could not believe what they were seeing. People were rooted to the spot and Lestrade and I were effectively blocked from getting closer. Past the man unconsciously impeding my progress I could see Allan's piteous face. If he could have reproduced the expressions that flitted across it to order, the man would have been the finest actor who ever lived. Sadness, pain, fear came and went as he looked at the face of the woman he'd come so far to kill. Then, in a flash, they were hustled off stage to make way for the dark side of his complex mind.

With a guttural roar he somehow leapt on to the railing, looked down on the Queen and with a cry of "How now, sweet queen! One woe doth tread upon another's heel!" he struck downward.

My next image is of the foil flying upwards,

twisting and turning, catching the light like some latter-day Excalibur, until it struck one of the wooden beams, where it hung, quivering gently.

I looked back to the lower gallery and couldn't believe my eyes. Allan had fallen back on to the yard floor and stood there, nursing a wrist that was obviously broken. But that was not what rivetted every eye. It was the Queen rising from her seat— and then continuing to rise until she stood at a height that far exceeded that of a diminutive little woman. In her hand was the silver topped stick she had leaned on when she entered—now revealed as a fearsome sword stick. It was this weapon that had so effectively disarmed Allan a moment earlier.

I could stand it no longer. Brandishing my revolver, I caused the man in front of me to move hastily aside. A moment later I had Allan pinioned with his hands behind him, while Lestrade slipped on the handcuffs. "You're safe now, Ma'am," I heard myself say and even to my ears the words sounded foolish.

"I'm most relieved to hear it, Watson," Her Majesty replied. And with that she put her hand to her head and pulled off the wig and mantilla. "It is no joke when a tall man has to take a foot off his height for an extended period of time. Try to dissuade me from doing so in the future, except under the direst of circumstances, there's a good fellow," said Sherlock Holmes.

Chapter Fifteen

So many questions were bubbling in my mind that I hardly knew which to ask first. "What do you suppose will happen to that poor fellow, Allan ... Lowe ... whatever his name was? I shall never forget the empty look on his face as Lestrade's men took him off."

"I sincerely hope he will get the best attention our primitive medical resources can provide," my friend replied, "but I have to admit to not being wildly optimistic. As Sigmund points out, the human mind is the last great frontier to be explored and our maps are rudimentary at best. Even he—as I'm sure he would be the first to admit—is but charting the foothills. If we knew but a fraction of its mysteries, I venture to suggest we could solve most of our cases without leaving the portals of Baker Street."

We were strolling along the river walk just beyond the Globe with the evening sun warming our faces. Behind us we could hear the sound of an appreciative new Elizabethan audience. How different a sound might there have been throughout the Empire and indeed the rest of the civilised world tonight but for the man walking at my side, dressed now in his familiar ulster and deerstalker, worn as if to assert his own identity. I had a sense that even he wished to put recent events firmly behind him and inhabit once more the comfortable world of Victoria's England. The events of the past few days had been incredible, even by his standards— incredible and unsettling to be in the presence of so deranged a mind. Evil we had encountered often enough but here we had faced pity as well as terror.

"I presume that, when the time comes, you will call our little adventure something like 'The Shakespeare Globe Murders'?" Holmes looked at me quizzically. "Despite the fact that by far the most interesting part of the whole affair were a number of what will one day, I don't doubt, be referred to as Freudian complications."

"You may well be right, Holmes," I said, entering into the spirit of things, "but you must admit there were times when the bodies seemed to be piling up with the regularity of—of . . ."

"Of an Elizabethan tragedy? Quite so. But I think you'll agree, Watson, that it was necessary to—as *you* might say—fight fire with fire. The genesis of the case was in the theatre—or, should I say, in *a* theatre. Faced with an opponent who only saw things clearly and whose actions were motivated by the world of artifice, it seemed apparent to me from the first that the play was the thing wherein we'd catch the conscience—or at least the attention—of the killer. And so it proved, though I must admit only to you and not for your confounded story—that there were moments I doubted my plot would hold . . ."

I thought back to the scene in the yard of the Globe not more than an hour or so ago . . .

As Lestrade's men took an unresisting Allan from my custody, I spun the Inspector around, I'm afraid a trifle roughly. "Come along, Lestrade, how much of this did you know? And why couldn't you have confided in me?"

"Don't be too hard on poor Lestrade, Watson," Holmes interceded, as with Mycroft's help he shed his royal disguise and straightened his normal attire.

"Like the good public servant he has always been, he did precisely what I asked him, which was to be where he was and do what he did. Oh, and to accept that, whatever strange events may take place on the stage, that they were part of my plan." Then, seeing that the Inspector was safely out of ear shot, he added—"If there is one thing our friends in the constabulary are particularly good at it is following orders!"

It was then I realised that in the excitement of the events in the gallery, I had totally forgotten the drama I had witnessed on the stage. I turned but Holmes had read my mind. "A play within a play within a play, I'm afraid. We had to provoke Allan or live in the certain knowledge that some time, somewhere he would erupt into violence. Where better than on a platform specifically devised for such actions?"

"But Carlotta . . . and Phipps?" By this time I had the answer to both questions. Phipps was being bandaged for what, even from a distance, I could see was no more than a flesh wound, while Carlotta was sitting in Gertrude's chair on the stage, receiving the attentive care of— Edward Alleyn!

"I doubt that Florenz Adler will ever give a finer performance," Holmes murmured at my shoulder. "I really think we should go over and congratulate him." As we climbed on to the stage and approached them, I saw that Tallis was also close by the two of them. They might not be a family in the true sense but I had a distinct feeling that recent events had created a bond that many true families never manage to forge and I was happy for them.

"Well, Mr Holmes, we pulled it off," said Adler, pale behind his make up. "I must admit, I had a nasty moment or two back there, stuck on that platform. I had no idea *why* I was doing what I was doing any more. I knew I was following your direction but it felt pretty creepy being directed from the grave—or so I thought. Next time I have a director, I want him where I can *see* him. And what about this little lady?"— and he put an arm around his wife's shoulders— "she clinched it. When she fell to the ground,

I could almost believe she *had* been poisoned."

"Make that two of us," said Carlotta. "I knew something strange was going on but I was brought up to believe that, when you're on stage, you say your lines and try not to bump into things."

"But," I interrupted, "I *saw* Allan put something in the wine."

"Quite right, Watson," said Holmes, "so you did. An exotic foreign substance called—cocoa powder. It could not do the lady the slightest harm—unless, of course, she happens to be allergic to cocoa."

Seeing that the explanation did not fully convince me, he continued—"Between us Lestrade's men and I shadowed Allan from the moment it was clear that he and only he could be the perpetrator of these literary happenings. When he made his decisive move to obtain poison—with, I might add, a very cleverly forged prescription—I was on hand. A very anxious cleric had very little trouble in persuading the chemist that he may have given to his young curate in error a prescription intended to remove mice from the vestry and then rushing off to correct his addle-pated error. It really is amazing how unquestioningly we trust the Church." And for a moment he took on the look of the befuddled vicar.

"Once we knew his intent—and knowing the scene that was to be enacted, that was simple enough to deduce. It was, in his mind, of course, the only scene he intended to be played. After that, well, I rather think that this is your part of the story . . ." He turned to Phipps, who had now joined us, his wounded arm in a sling and the other around Pauline French, who had hurried from backstage, looking beautifully incongruous—and incongruously beautiful as Katharine of France for the *Henry V* that was to follow.

"Nothing much to tell, really," Phipps replied, his attention more on Miss French than on the rest of us—and who could blame him? "I just followed Inspector Lestrade's suggestion. I shared a dressing cubicle with Allan," he added by way of clarification. "It was easy enough to go through his things and there was this folder of paper with some brown powder in it. So . . ." He shrugged his shoulders, "I substituted one lot of brown powder for another. Then I threw that first lot down the sink pretty darn quickly, I can assure you!"

"Which was just as well for me," said Carlotta from her seat. "Of course, Flo brought me in on the game just before he 'disappeared' but, as the moment in the scene came nearer, I had no way of knowing whether Simon had managed to do his substitution trick. I have to say I don't think I've acted better, not even when we did *The Ring* at the Met."

"Your *second* finest hour, my dear," said Edward Alleyn, as I was now coming to think of Adler. "And I do believe, modestly, that I myself have never done better since—oh, since . . ."

"*Our American Cousin?*" his wife asked teasingly. "At least this performance ended with the audience intact, even if the players were a little the worse for wear. If you go on like this, Flo, people will soon ask to be insured before they come to an Adler show!"

She smiled when she realised that he hadn't heard a word. Friend Adler hadn't got where he was by listening to things he didn't want to hear. Right now he was reliving his own part. "Yes, I have to admit I felt the old thrill standing there. You know, I *might* try Lear one of these days, what do you think, Lotta?" Then, taking in the audience for the first time, he exclaimed— "My God, we've got a show to do! What must all these people think?"

"Mr Adler," Holmes said reassuringly, "I suggest they will think whatever you tell them to think. They came to see an unexpected spectacle and even the most mean-spirited can hardly dispute that they have already had their money's worth. I would be inclined to tell them that you were staging an experimental drama and wished to see whether a modern audience would react with the true spontaneity of its Elizabethan forebears."

So Adler did just that. And while the audience was settling down and buzzing with the excitement of what they would tell their families and friends when they returned home, the rest of us exited stage left, as I believe it is called, to the relative peace of the actors' dressing rooms.

"Well, Watson," said Holmes, turning to me, "I have never been good at goodbyes, so I propose we take a quiet stroll and leave these good people to their several devices. That will give us ample time to be back in Baker Street for what, I have reason to believe, will to be one of Mrs Hudson's special dinners." He answered my unspoken question. "Don't worry, her mind was put at rest the moment you left Baker Street."

"Just before you go, Mr Holmes,"—it was Carlotta—"may I thank both of you for all you've done? I know it sounds a funny thing to say after what's just happened but a few days ago I was drifting and now I know where I'm going. I've rediscovered a few things I thought I'd lost . . ." She paused and in the silence we could hear Adler's distinctive voice on stage. From the laughter and applause he was managing his audience effortlessly. Carlotta put her hand on Tallis's arm and continued. "And I've found a few I never knew I had. And if there's anything I can do to help that other young man, when . . ."

"I'm sure there will be, Mrs Adler. One of these days we shall understand the human mind a lot better than we do today. Great strides are being made by Freud and others and—who knows?—it's not impossible, given time, that they may find a way to drive out those malevolent elements that are preying on your . . ." He sought for the word . . . "your young colleague. You must hold on to the fact that it was not he who did these things. Watson and I will to be sure to keep you informed. Right, Watson?" I mumbled something by way of agreement. I've never been good at dealing with a lot of emotion and the room was full of it.

Now it was Pauline French's turn. "If we're swapping exit lines, Mr Holmes, may I have one? What's going to happen to Simon?" And she clutched that young man's good arm protectively.

"I imagine he may be promoted to play Hamlet and receive rather good notices from the gentlemen of the press," Holmes replied with a vestigial twinkle in his eye.

"Please, Mr Holmes, you know what I mean."

Holmes looked at something about six inches above her left shoulder, an experience that was probably new to her. "I believe the police are having problems with the description of Allan's companion on the night of Fiske's demise. Apparently, it would fit just about any of several hundred thousand young men. Then again, I doubt that an inadequate masquerade in clerical garb ranks as a misdemeanour, let alone a crime . . ."

and for the briefest of moments the rubicund cleric took him over again. "No Miss French, I fancy the services Mr Phipps has rendered recently will more than compensate for any earlier—shall we say—indiscretions." Then, looking firmly at Phipps: "A man who fails to learn from his mistakes would do well to consider *himself* a mistake." Phipps brightened immediately and for the first time looked my friend in the eye. "Wilde?" he asked. "No. Holmes. Good day to you all." A few moments later and the wooden "O" was behind us for the last time.

I looked for signs of the lassitude that invariably enveloped Holmes once a case was over. So far it seemed to have held off. We walked along in companionable silence for a while longer and then I could contain myself no longer.

"Holmes, why couldn't you have told me? You must have some idea of what I've been through these past few hours?"

He stopped, put his hands on both my shoulders and turned me round to face him. There was no argument with the expression on his face. "Watson, you were the one person I could not tell. Your total and transparent sincerity was my trump card. It was imperative that word got back to Allan that I was really out of the picture in the most finite possible way. He had a competitor, someone dangerous enough to kill the redoubtable

Sherlock Holmes. If there was any possibility of remorse or normal reaction, it might be possible to shock him back to a form of sanity—at least for long enough to let us get safely past the opening and to give Lestrade enough time to collect evidence to bring charges.

"Frankly, I was not optimistic—particularly after hearing Sigmund's opinion—and, as it turned out the dementia was too far advanced. That being the case, I had to be ready to provoke his madness and deal with it. It looked dangerous, to be sure, but in logic there was only one course open to him . . ."

"To kill the Queen?"

"To kill what he thought was the Queen."

"But what about last night, Holmes? I know all about Pauline French. But you were dead on that stage. I saw you lying there with my own eyes . . ."

"No, Watson, I arranged it so that what you saw was the improbable not the impossible. You had the vital clue in your own words."

"My own words?" I must have looked like the Idiot Boy.

"Do you remember a little tale I believe you called 'The Empty Room'?"

"In it you chronicled my return from the so-called 'dead' after the Moriarty affair at Reichenbach, pursued by one Colonel Sebastian Moran . . ."

"The 'second most dangerous man in London,' you called him."

"The very same. Moriarty's lieutenant. I lured him into believing he could shoot me as I sat at my Baker Street window from the empty house opposite but you will recall that his target turned out to be . . ."

"A wax bust!"

"The work of Monsieur Oscar Meunier of Grenoble—and an excellent piece of work it was. So much so that—and it's possible I omitted to inform you of this—I had Monsieur Meunier execute a full figure dummy, just in case I had subsequent need of it. That was what you saw on the stage of the Globe last night. I'm afraid the sandbag caused a certain amount of unavoidable damage but, considering the alternative as a means of creating verisimilitude, I fancy it as the preferred option . . ."

"But what about the fellow up in the gallery? The chap I fired at?"

"You very nearly succeeded in bringing my plans to a rather premature conclusion there, old fellow. That was me and you only just missed me. I had just had the rare satisfaction of arranging my own death, in a manner of speaking, and lingered a moment too long to admire my own handiwork. Frankly, I had assumed Miss French's Ophelia might have detained you all a few moments longer. By the way, wasn't she admirable? I can think of few women—well, perhaps *one*—who would have been as spirited as she.

"Nonetheless, Watson, *you* were the true star of my little drama. And I must confess, it was the way that you reacted to my previous 'departure' that gave me the idea. Forgive me, old friend— I give you my word that this is the last time I shall employ that particular stratagem."

His gaze was fixed on the opposite side of the river as he added—"By the way, I meant every word in my note. In more ways than you can possibly know you define me."

I knew that the subject was effectively closed. We walked on in silence for several minutes before I said—in a tone I hoped would convey that I bore no resentment—"A penny for them, Holmes."

He looked at me almost apologetically, I thought. "I'm afraid the Bard was on my mind, Watson, as he has been so much of late. 'What manner of man?' as he so presciently asked. In this play we have so recently witnessed and in which we have played our humble parts, have we not experienced so many of the motivations, the pain and the joy he chronicled so well? Who knows, perhaps from some celestial prompt corner he even orchestrated the whole thing."

"Well, if he did, I sincerely hope his celestial audience knew more about the plot than I did,"

I said and had the satisfaction of seeing a rare touch of embarrassment cross Holmes's face. If I had hoped for a more formal apology, I was not about to receive one. Instead, half to himself, I heard him say . . .

Our revels now are ended. These our
   actors—
As I foretold you—were all spirits and
Are melted into air, into thin air;
And like the baseless fabric of this vision
The cloud-capp'd towers, the gorgeous
   palaces,
The solemn temples . . .

He paused, then continued . . .

. . . the great globe itself
Yes, all which it inherit, shall dissolve
And like this insubstantial pageant faded
Leave not a wrack behind . . .

"But not, I trust, for at least *another* three hundred years, eh Watson?"

We walked a little further and then I asked him a question that had been bothering me. "Holmes, when we left the actors, you went back to the yard. I couldn't help notice the group that came in that you were talking to. Wasn't Mycroft one of them?"

"Quite right, old fellow. You saw and you *did*

observe. Surely you didn't expect Her Majesty to miss the first performance at the Globe?"

"That was the *Queen?*"

"Most certainly. She had observed my performance from the seclusion of one of the boxes and was good enough to compliment me on the dignity of my bearing." He threw his head back and laughed loudly, causing several passers by to turn and stare.

"And was that all she said?" I prompted.

Holmes thought a moment, knowing the meaning of my question. "Come to think of it, there was a mention of some trifling honour. I'm afraid Mycroft has a bee in his bonnet about it. Which fortunately, gave me the clue."

"And what did you say?"

"I thanked Her Majesty for the kind thought and suggested that, should she find me worthy in my next career, I should be pleased and honoured to accept."

"Your *next* career?"

"I told her I intended to retire to the Sussex Downs and keep bees."

"And what did she say?"

"She seemed quite amused."

Center Point Large Print
600 Brooks Road / PO Box 1
Thorndike, ME 04986-0001 USA

(207) 568-3717

US & Canada:
1 800 929-9108
www.centerpointlargeprint.com